Helen Wilkinson is the author of *Dying to Live, The Missing Peace* and the acclaimed best-seller *Peter's Daughter*. She was born in 1962, educated in Warwick and at London University, and now lives in Shrewsbury with her husband and daughter.

Also by Helen Wilkinson;

Dying to Live

The Missing Peace

Peter's Daughter

CHINKS

One boy's search for a Dad and a dog.

A NOVEL BY

Helen Wilkinson

Stickleback books

CHINKS

A STICKLEBACK BOOK

Published in England 2005 by Stickleback Books
an imprint of Ichthus Ltd
10 Park Plaza
Battlefield Industrial Estate
Shrewsbury, SY1 3AF

ISBN 0-9543105-2-7

Printed and bound in Great Britain by Biddles Ltd
Cover photograph Tal-y-llyn Lake © Jeremy Moore www.wild-wales.com
Cover design by River Media

www.sticklebackbooks.com
Email: sales@sticklebackbooks.com

Written for
my Godsons with love;
Peter, Matthew, Sebastian
and Joe.

Toby,
we were always meant to be
together.

If you're going to read my story, you've got to promise me two things - first that you won't laugh at me, because it isn't easy to talk about. OK?

Number two - you won't feel sorry for me. Because I'm all right.

Here goes.

I don't have a Dad.

And I don't mean that I had a Dad but he's divorced, or died, or that I don't know who he is, no, I actually don't have one.

Are you laughing? Good. And I don't need you to feel sorry either. I just don't have a Dad.

I found out when I was five or six. One lunch break in Year 2, Peter Pike told me his Mum and Dad were divorced.

Immediately I began to wonder if the same had happened to my family. That night, when Mum had finished reading me a bedtime story, I asked her, 'Are you divorced from my Dad?'

'You don't have a Dad.'

'But everyone has a Dad.'

'Well you don't.'

Mum paused for a moment and looked at my Bart curtains, as if she was seeing through them and needed an answer from somewhere.

I tried again, 'Well where did I come from then?'

'My tummy.'

'So how did I get in?'

'I'll tell you when you're older.'

Last week I was fourteen, and I figured that makes me old enough to know the truth, so I planned to ask Mum in the car on the way back from rugby club. I looked at her sideways in the driver's seat beside me, at her short dark hair, pale face and thin hands. She always looks worried, tense, as if now is definitely not the right time to ask for something.

I'd spent ages planning the best way to ask the question. I waited till we were out of the car park, then swallowed hard and spoke, 'Mum, ages ago, you promised to tell me about my Dad when I was older.' I held my breath and prepared for a long wait.

'You don't have a Dad.'

And she never even paused before this answer, as if she'd had the words on the tip of her tongue for the last eight years, just waiting for me to ask.

I looked out of the car window at the familiar town view flashing past; Tesco car park, Tesco petrol station, Tesco superstore. Slow down for the traffic lights. Stare at geeky boy in the Ford Focus next to me at the lights. Stick tongue out without Mum seeing. Pull off. Pass Bert the Butcher's, Post Office, row of boring houses, bus stop.

I took a deep breath and tried not to be embarrassed. This is NOT the kind of thing you discuss with your parents, 'Mum, I've done about reproduction and pregnancy at school and I know where babies come from.'

I knew that would shock her, 'And everyone must have a Dad.'

'Well you don't.'

'This isn't fair. Why won't you tell me?'

'You have no father.' She said this in the kind of voice she uses when I ask for a new football kit, or an iPod. Not the

'We'll see' tone, but the 'If-you-don't-be-quiet-I'll-be-furious' voice.

So I shut up and tried to squash the anger down inside my stomach. It sort of didn't fit, and bits of it kept popping up into my throat and head. Bits of anger that said, 'Of course I've got a Dad. Why won't she tell me?'

So I tried thinking of something else, and imagined I was Jonny Wilkinson. The entire England squad was waiting for me to kick the ball squarely between the posts. The score 35/34 to France, one minute to the final whistle. Everything depended on my boot.

I drew my leg back.

Mum interrupted my moment, 'But you're about to have a step-dad.'

'You what?'

'Don't say what - say pardon.'

This can't be good news. Wanting to know about my real Dad is one thing, but suddenly finding out I'm getting a step-dad is not what I had in mind. Not at all.

I don't know why Mum suddenly chose to mention it. I was worried she may think it's a way of making up to me for not answering my question, so I decided to play it safe, 'It's OK Mum, I can live without a Dad. You don't have to get me a step-dad. I'd prefer to stay as we are.'

'Joel, For the last fourteen years, I've struggled to make ends meet. Raising a child is very expensive.'

'I'm sorry, I'll stop going on about wanting an iPod.' I paused for a second after making this massive sacrifice, and added, 'Or an X box.'

'Oh love, I can't afford to get you a cardboard box, never mind an X box.'

This time I wasn't seeing the houses and shops as they flashed by. I was trying to get used to the idea that I'll always be the only boy at Ryton High who doesn't have a play-station, or iPod. I have Mum's old mobile - it's a Motorola brick - and I'm too embarrassed to take it to school.

I weighed the facts up in my head, and decided I'd rather have Mum without the money, than have a step-dad.

'Is he rich?'

'He's going to be.'

My ears pricked up. This might be worth a few more questions, 'What sort of car does he have?'

'A Peugeot 205.'

'Customised?'

'You know it's pointless asking me about cars love, it's

red, and very sweet, and he's had it for ages.'

'So it isn't customised then.' My hopes were fading fast.

She added, 'Well I think he had it in 1989.'

'So it's older than me. That reeks! Forget it. I don't want a step-dad.'

'Joel, it isn't up to you. You're going to meet him on Sunday at Gran's. And Davey and I are planning to get married - soon.'

'Davey! - what kind of a name's Davey?'

'It's from David, Dave... Davey. Please don't take this attitude Joel. Don't make it any more difficult for me than it is already.'

This time I said it under my breath, 'Davey, Davey, what a pathetic name for a man.'

Usually I look forward to Sunday lunch at Granny Wen's. Mum's mother is really fashionable and cool. She looks about the same age as my Mum - which is pretty weird - and sometimes people mistake them for sisters. This makes Gran-Wen laugh her head off, but makes my Mum really grumpy.

Gran-Wen wears boiler suits when she's working - she's an engineer - and Tommy Hilfiger tee-shirts when she's at home with Gramps. That's my Grandad.

He's a house-husband - he cooks the supper, cleans their house, and does the food shopping. He thinks this is fine, but you won't catch me doing it, even when I'm ancient like him.

So Gran-Wen has all the fun going out to work and being an engineer, restoring old steam engines and vintage cars and stuff like that. She learned engineering millions of years ago when women were supposed to be secretaries and teachers, and Mum says she was dead proud of her Mum when she was my age.

Gran-Wen still has wavy fair hair which she ties up loosely when she goes out to work, and she wears no make-up. All the blokes still fancy her. She won't allow the men to swear when she's in the workshop, and Gramps says they're terrified of her. But she's funny, and has twice as much energy as most other people.

Sunday lunch at Gran's is a highlight of the week, but this time, the fear of meeting Davey almost put me off the thought of Gramps' famous roast chicken dinner. Almost.

I offered to walk the few hundred metres from our house to Gran's, while Mum went to pick up Davey. It's one of the main things I love about living in town, being so near to Gran, and the cinema and the surfing shops.

It was cold and windy as I walked down our street, round the corner, and up the much nicer road that leads to Gran's. Despite the winter weather, their garden looked perfectly neat. Gramps came to the door in his pinny, his round face beaming, bald head shining, and he hugged me tight, 'How's my favourite grandson?' He says that every time we meet.

I checked to make sure no-one had seen the embarrassing hug, and tried to direct him inside away from prying eyes, 'I'm Your only grandson, ' I replied, going through the old routine.

'Still my favourite!' Gramps joked as he hung up my fleece. The warm, cosy smell of dinner and clean house started to make me feel better about meeting Davey.

'Wotcha Joel!' called Gran-Wen as she galloped down the stairs, two at a time.

'Hi Gran.'

She gave me a bear-hug, 'Hey tinker - don't call me Gran. My name's Wendy, how many times do I have to remind you?'

Gran-Wen hates being called Gran. She thinks she's too young.

'Sorry Gran-Wen.'

She tilted my chin and examined my up-turned face carefully, 'Are you all right Jo-Jo?'

'Ish.'

'Time for a family conference,' she insisted, steering me down the hall towards the big warm kitchen at the back of the house, 'Put your pan down Nigel, this is important.'

Gramps wiped his hands and came to the big pine table.

Gran-Wen pulled out three chairs. 'So what's the matter Jo-Jo, we can't have you upset. Is it school?'

'No, school's great, I got a credit award this week.'

'Well done mate, well done,' nodded Gramps, 'What's a credit award?'

'Nigel, you're the limit,' Gran frowned. She turned to me, 'So what is it love? You can tell us.'

I had thought about this moment a thousand times before. It was a risk, a big risk, but I know Gran-Wen and Gramps love me, so I went for it, 'Why does Mum say I haven't got a Dad?'

Gramps was lifting his coffee mug to his lips. He stopped - mug half way to mouth, his arm frozen in mid air. Gran-Wen looked from him to me, and back to him again, and her eyes were wide and stare-y.

Neither of them said anything, so I went on, 'And that's bad enough, but now Mum tells me I'm getting a step-dad. And his name's Davey. How tragic is that?'

Gramps let out his breath slowly, in a thin whistly line, but didn't speak.

'Well, yes, we're about to meet him ourselves,' said Gran-Wen, 'And I guess he can't help his name.'

Under his breath Gramps said to Gran, 'You try calling me Nigey and I'll thump you.'

'Be quiet Nigel!' Gran-Wen sounded very cross, which is really rare for her, 'Joel, I think your mother has had a tough time over the years.'

'Am I that bad?' I asked.

She reached across the table and squeezed my shoulder, 'Oh I didn't mean that, you're a star - the best son and grandson anyone ever had. You're no trouble, and very good-natured.'

'And lazy,' Gramps added, smiling.

She went on, 'And, between the three of us, and these four walls, your mother has always had a bit of a problem with - well, men.'

'What do you mean?'

Gran-Wen paused, 'She finds them, a bit..... tricky.'

'Hates them you mean,' said Gramps under his breath again.

Gran-Wen turned on him, 'If you have nothing positive to say Nigel, then get back to your oven!'

An outburst from Gran-Wen is so unusual that Gramps looked stunned, 'Sorry Wen, truly am. But this business about Davey is as big a bombshell for me as for young Joel here. But I don't mean to make the situation any worse than it is. I'll just check my chicken.' He looked gutted.

'Thank you,' Gran-Wen said, and turned her chair to face me square on. She looked worried and caring at the same time. 'The question about your Dad, or lack of him, is something you need to talk about with Mum. But Davey is someone we're all going to try and like, and if he gives you any bother, you just phone us, and we'll come and collect you. In fact, have my mobile number,' Gran-Wen said, tearing a piece off the kitchen notepad, and scribbling quickly.

'Don't worry Gran, I can always walk, however bad things get, I can always wait 'til after school and come and tell you then.'

Gran-Wen turned her head and looked at Gramps again, with the same wide open eyes.

'So she hasn't told him,' Gramps said quietly.

'Told me what?'

Just then the key turned in the front door and we heard Mum calling cheerfully, 'Hello you lot. We're here!'

You know on a film when they make the picture slow motion, usually when someone's being shot or run over? And everything is silent and well - slow. That's exactly how this moment was.

My ears went deaf and I stopped hearing the noise from the oven, or the music on Gramps' CD, or anything. I turned my head and saw Mum and this bloke walking very slowly through the hall towards the kitchen.

Very, very slowly Gran-Wen got up from the table and walked towards them in slow-mo, holding out her hand.

Then the noise of a Sunday kitchen burst in again, and everything returned to normal speed. 'Hello, hello, nice to meet you,' the four adults were all saying at once.

'Windy outside isn't it?'

'Yes, no sign of spring yet.'

The usual sort of nonsense adults talk. Their conversation seems to be like the first few passes in a game of football, not very impressive, as if they're working out what the other team are going to do first.

Teenagers aren't like that - we just burst out with what's important straight away; 'Danny O'Donoghue's little brother wet himself in PE.' That sort of thing.

Today I went straight to the important thing too, never mind if Davey was there or not, 'Mum, what is it you haven't told me that means I won't be able to come round to Gran-Wen's after school?'

The four adults went stony silent.

Mum frowned and lowered her voice, speaking each word separately, 'Joel. Don't. Start.'

Then she put her hand on Davey's arm and smiled cheesily at me, 'Come and say hello to Davey properly love.'

I looked at him for the first time. Slightly taller than Mum, tanned in an orange-y way, quite slim but absolutely ancient. Really unbelievably grey haired.

I stood up from the table and moved one step towards

him, 'How old are you?' I asked.

'Joel!' shouted Mum.

Gramps burst out laughing, then covered his mouth and turned to look out of the window.

Davey's eyes were glinting angrily as he smiled at Mum in a totally slimy way. Then he laughed a 'Huh, huh,' kind of laugh which meant - *I don't think this is at all funny but I need to look cool.*

'Well well,' he said to Mum, 'Your son's pretty direct'. Then he looked at me very suspiciously, 'I'm a few years older than your mother, and wearing well. The squash keeps me fit.'

'That's how we met,' gushed Mum, 'At the gym. Davey's the best squash coach at the sports centre, and he started to give me extra lessons. That's some six-pack!' she said, patting him on the front of his England shirt.

He put his hand on top of hers.

I noticed a gold band on one of his fingers. 'Are you married?' I asked him.

Gramps started to fiddle noisily with pans on his cooker.

Davey's reaction was a winner. He looked down at his hand and kind of jumped, as if he'd just been bitten by a flea. Then he twisted and pulled his ring off and put it in his pocket.

It was all too much for Mum, she grabbed me by the arm and dragged me upstairs into her old bedroom, (which is now the spare room), and shut the door.

Once it was closed, she started shouting, but under her breath - so the others wouldn't hear. Pointless I know, because it was pretty obvious she hadn't taken me out for a squash lesson, ha ha.

'How dare you, how dare you? For the last fourteen years all I've ever done is slave over you, body and soul, worrying about your future, washing your socks and living my life through yours. And now for the first time in years I've found a man I could love, and I've brought him home and this is how you repay me. It simply won't do Joel.' She ran out of steam and threw my arm down, rubbing her head with her hands distractedly.

'But he's married,' I said bluntly.

'WAS married. He's getting divorced. It was just a simple mistake, forgetting to take off his ring, he hasn't lived with his ex-wife for ages. So you just go downstairs and apologise to him right now, and never, ever behave like that again, or....'

'Or what?'

'Or I'll tan your backside, that's what.'

She opened the bedroom door and Davey was standing outside on the landing.

'Hi,' she managed, weakly.

I pushed past him and legged it downstairs, pausing underneath the banisters just in case I overheard anything interesting. I regret that, because what I heard next made me pretty confused.

Although she'd just told me it was fine that Davey had forgotten to take off his ring, straight away I heard Mum snap at him, 'What the hell does this mean? What's that thing doing on your finger? You've been with HER haven't you?'

I trudged into the kitchen and stood looking at Gran-Wen and Gramps. Why do adults tell so many lies? And why do they try and kid themselves all the time?

At least Gran-Wen and Gramps don't do that. It suddenly occurred to me that's why they're different - they're always real with me. Always straight.

Gran-Wen stepped forward and squeezed me into her

arms, 'Joel, everything will be OK. We love you, the boat's going to rock a bit, but the storm will pass.'

'Yeah hold on mate,' Gramps added.

It wasn't the most fun Sunday lunch I've ever had. Understatement of the century.

As we sat round the dining room table, Gran-Wen and Gramps tried to cheer things along. Mum looked pale and was much quieter than usual, she smiled a lot, but they were weak, flat smiles, nothing like the ones she smiles at home when we're watching *Little Britain*. And Davey showed off.

Most new adults ask me loads of questions. I'm sure it's happened to you too. Questions like, 'So, are you enjoying school?'

Bet if I answered back, 'So, are you enjoying your job?' they'd think I was downright cheeky and I'd be told off. So how come it's OK for them to ask me?

Another favourite is, 'What do you want to do when you grow up?' How personal is that? They've only just met me and they're asking deep private questions. I don't even talk to Mum about my plans for the future. And the adults wonder why I clam up and look at the floor and don't seem very interested in replying to their questions.

Well, Davey didn't bother with any of that stuff. In fact he didn't bother with me at all. He tried very hard to impress Gran-Wen and Gramps, and of course he slimed all over Mum, but he acted as if I wasn't there. And I did the same back. So our step-son/step-dad relationship hasn't got off to a brilliant start.

And the signs are all bad - he doesn't like football, only squash and tennis. He's old. He's already got kids. They're grown up so they won't matter much, but it brings a whole lot of other people into the situation who aren't invited.

When it was time to leave, Gran-Wen gave me a special squeeze and whispered in my ear, 'Be brave Jo-Jo, we're on the end of a phone.'

I didn't say a single word all the way to Davey's house as I sat in the back of our car. I was shoved in the back so HE could sit in front next to Mum.

We didn't see his actual house because he insisted on being dropped at the end of his road. They almost had a row about that, not a shouting one, but a quiet adult row.

It started when Mum said, 'I'll drop you at the house, it's raining.'

'No, here will be fine thanks.'

'Why don't you want me to take you to the house?'

'Don't start Caitlin.'

'She's in the house isn't she?'

'We've been over this. I'll call you tonight.'

'If you can tear yourself away.'

They didn't speak again and Davey slammed the car door hard as he got out. He didn't wave.

As soon as we'd driven off, Mum grabbed her mobile from her handbag and tried ringing him over and over again, as if she was panicking that she'd been cross.

Throughout the journey home I kept complete silence in the back of the car. All I wanted was to be as far away from the tension as possible, longing for my room, where I hid from the inevitable talk with Mum.

I didn't have long to wait.

She knocked at my door. Mum never knocks unless it's something important. When she comes to fetch dirty washing or wake me up she doesn't knock.

'Joel, can I come in?'

I stayed quiet.

She pushed the door gently and came and sat at the end of my bed, holding a glass of wine. She looked awful - tired and sad, but I was not going to show any sympathy.

I carried on watching my TV determinedly.

'Can we turn that off for a minute?' she asked.

I leaned forward and pressed the red button. I hate these kind of moments. As a rule it's best to keep quiet.

'I've been sitting downstairs planning to come up and give you a telling off for being so rude today.'

'I WAS **NOT** RUDE!' I shouted.

'Hush, I haven't finished. I was *going* to tell you off, but I can't. Because I realised that actually, you didn't do anything wrong. Today was really tough for you, and I want to explain a few things.'

'Can I watch the telly now?'

'In a minute love.'

Mum took a sip of wine and looked thoughtful, 'You guessed right about Davey being married. But he will be getting divorced and he's going to live with us.'

'Live with us?' This was worse than I thought.

'Yes. And we'll get married one day.' Suddenly she looked worried, 'But don't mention that bit to Davey yet - the bit about marriage. He's been so nice to me, he makes me feel young again, and I'm sure you'll grow to like him more as time goes by.'

There was no point responding to such an idiotic statement.

'Joel, we've always had good times together haven't we?'

'Yes, so why bring Davey in to mess it up?'

'Because I'm lonely.'

'Why are you lonely when you've got me?'

'I need a partner, like other Mums have, and you won't

always be here. It won't be long until you go to college and I'll be on my own. Davey makes me feel good about myself.....
and he thinks I'm pretty.'

'I think you're pretty.'

'Oh love,' she said, and hugged me. She's being a pain right now over Davey, but basically she's a good Mum. We've had fun times together and she's never given me too much grief. Until now.

'TV?' I asked again.

'It's time to tell you why you won't be able to go to Granny Wen's after school.'

I stopped moving. Stopped breathing. If this involved Davey I knew it couldn't be good news.

Mum put her arm round me absent-mindedly and had another sip of wine, 'Davey needs to make a fresh start now he's getting divorced, and he needs to get away from his old life. Move away from the places that remind him of his ex-wife.'

So Davey's moving - hurray!

'And he's full of brilliant ideas, that's one of the things I like about him. Because he won't have much money after the divorce, he's going to start his own business. And, I'm going to start it with him.'

'Where?'

Mum's expression flickered from hopeful to hopeless, 'Wales.'

'But that's miles away isn't it?'

'Up to the middle of England, then turn left.'

'How can you and Davey get there every morning from here?'

'No Joel, were moving to Wales. All of us.'

I felt as if I'd been hit in the stomach with the rugby ball,

'I'm not moving.'

'We'll find a lovely house in the countryside and have a few hens and a goat.'

'And a dog. Can I have a dog?'

'Maybe. Wales is beautiful.'

'I hate the countryside. I love it here.' Then the awful realisation hit me, 'What about Gran-Wen and Gramps? Are they coming with us?'

Mum paused and swallowed her last mouthful of wine, 'No Jo-Jo, they can't leave Staines. Gran-Wen loves her job. So they'll stay here, but they'll come and visit us often.'

She jumped off the bed, excited suddenly, 'I've got a video to show you about the new business Davey and I are going to be running. Come and watch it with me.'

I stood up, feeling and moving like a robot. The last thing I wanted to do right now was go and watch some useless, boring video about Davey. But Mum was urging me, beckoning me with her hand and smiling with excitement.

So I trudged downstairs and waited as she tried to put the video into the player. As usual, after a minute she turned to me, 'Could you do it love?'

It happens every Friday when we hire a video to watch together.

I un-set the timer, ejected the blank tape, this isn't rocket science, but Mum can't get the hang of it at all.

I pressed PLAY and the video began.

Mum sat beside me, 'Don't fast forward, it starts straight away.'

The video stank. It reeked.

There was a whole lot of stuff about money and dreams - with seagulls flying about with tacky music playing. And a man's voice in an American accent asking if you're happy with your life, and how this video will help you seize your dreams. As I say, it stank.

I stopped listening after the first few minutes. There was one bit which nearly got interesting, with a girl in a bikini putting sun-cream on, but it didn't last long.

Then it went on some more about targets, building your business, and how you can expect to make a hundred thousand pounds in your first year.

At the end Mum turned to me proudly, 'What did you think?'

'I didn't understand it.'

'You will. When we get to Wales.'

'If we go to Wales, can I have a dog?'

'Davey hates dogs.'

Have you ever seen that episode of *The Simpsons* when Bart keeps on nagging Homer for something he wants?

I saw that episode, and never forgot it. All the way through, Bart keeps demanding, and Homer keeps replying 'No', until they're arguing so fast you can hardly hear them. Bart knows he'll wear his Dad down in the end. And his Dad kind of knows it too.

I've found this a very useful tactic. If you go on about something long enough, eventually you wear your parents down. It's a good idea to ask for the thing you want when they're tired or busy. That way they hardly notice, and you may get them to say 'yes' without them realising. There is a potential problem with this approach - later they may deny they ever said 'yes'. When they're less busy and thinking straight.

I decided to use the Bart/Homer tactic over a dog. Because the way I see it, if Mum's going to

a) drag me off to the middle of nowhere,

b) tear me away from my school, my friends and grandparents,

c) force me to live with a man I hate,

then I deserve a pay-back.

And I've always wanted a dog. Any dog. Brown, white, black or multi-coloured. As long as it's got four legs and wags its tail, I want it. Dogs are more reliable than humans, they don't give you grief, and they love you. All the time, even when you're bad.

My obsession with a dog started when I was really small and saw a film about a boy in Mexico who found a stray dog which was stuck in a disused mine shaft. The dog was wiry, brown and medium sized. He had shiny black eyes and a really waggy tail. In one scene the dog was trapped in the mine and his boy was calling down from the top. Don't laugh if I tell you this, but the dog looked so sad it nearly made me cry. He escaped of course - in case you're worried. I knew it would be all right too, but the dog's eyes still got to me.

Ever since seeing that film, I've longed for a dog. And I already know what I will call him. Not Fido or any other stupid dog name. I'll call my dog Chinks.

I found the name on a map of the Scilly Isles. Gran-Wen and Gramps took me on holiday there once. Best holiday I ever had. We flew on a helicopter, stayed in a cottage and went on millions of boat rides looking at seals and stuff. While we were on a boat trip to Round Island Lighthouse, I looked at Gramps' map to check our route. That's when I noticed the name - Chinks. It's the name of a pair of small rocks that are really close together in the water. Nearly touching.

I can understand why they called them Chinks, the rocks are so close they nearly chink together. And there are two of them. I knew right away that when I got my dog we'd be like the two rocks. Really close together but separate. Nearly touching, but not quite, meant to be together. If this doesn't make any sense, then you probably ought to stop reading this and try *The Lord of the Rings*.

The morning after the awful Sunday lunch with Davey, I began my campaign of wearing Mum down. The first thing I said at breakfast was, 'When are we moving to Wales?'

Mum looked pleased and replied, 'Very soon, probably Easter.'

'Can I have a dog.'

'Joel - I told you, Davey doesn't like dogs.'

'I don't care. I want a dog.'

'No, no, NO. No dog.'

'Last night you said maybe.'

'That was before you started making such a fuss.'

'Then I'm not coming to Wales.'

'Don't be ridiculous, of course you're coming.' Mum's voice was getting edgy.

'I'll only come if I can have a dog.'

I knew I was pushing my luck, and sure enough, Mum snapped, 'You'll do what you're damn-well told. Eat your breakfast and SHUT UP about a dog!'

So that was the end of round one.

After school I let myself in with my key as usual. When Mum came home I tried again, and as the angry approach hadn't got me anywhere, this time I decided to be upset instead.

'How was your day at school?' she asked.

'OK.'

'Did you tell your friends about moving?'

'No.'

'Why not?'

'Dunno, I just didn't.' I paused, then, 'Mum?'

'Yes love.'

I had thought this out carefully, 'I'm a bit upset about moving to Wales and it would be much nicer for me if I could look forward to having a dog.'

Mum stopped clearing the table for a second, and I knew I'd made an impact.

'I understand that moving house is a big shock for you Jo-Jo, but you'll realise in time that it's the best thing for all of us.'

She seemed to be focussing on me being upset, rather than on the dog bit. So I added, 'I could cope if I had a dog.'

Mum sighed very heavily and started to wash the dishes, 'Why don't you go and watch television?'

I knew this was her way of ending the conversation about the dog, so I decided to make the most of it, 'Can I go on the internet?'

'OK, but only for 15 minutes.'

I decided to ask her about the dog again at bedtime, and logged on to MSN.

Three weeks have gone by since I met Davey. And I've had about 96 conversations with Mum about the dog. Still no luck, but I haven't given up.

Yesterday was the pits. In form time, Mrs McGiven said she had some news for the class. I carried on flicking the back of Neil Morrison's hand with my plastic ruler.

'9G5, will you please settle down. The news I want to tell you is about Joel Tillyard.'

I stopped flicking and stared at Mrs McGiven. I wanted to disappear into the floor.

'Stand up Joel.'

Slowly, painfully, I pushed my chair back, heard it scrape along the floor, and stood in the middle of the form. I still had my ruler in my hand.

'Joel will be leaving us at the end of this term, won't you Joel? He's moving to Wales where his mother is setting up a new business. So Joel, I want to say good luck, and how we'll all miss you from this form. Won't we 9G5?'

A murmur of surprise went up from the form.

Then Neil Morrison flicked me really hard on the bum with his ruler.

I sat down without even kicking him.

Gemma and Ailsa turned round from the next table and whispered, 'Why you moving?' 'Wot's wrong with Staines?'

'Settle down, settle down,' went on Mrs McGiven. Who's got their form for Year 9 camp? Hand them in - if you've managed to remember them.'

And with a sickening thud, I realised I wouldn't be able to go to summer camp.

At break everyone gathered round me.

'You don't speak Welsh!'

'Why can't your Mum do her business in Staines?'

'No-one'll like you at your new school.'

'Shut up,' I shouted. 'I'm going to have a dog.'

Then the boys started a game of football and I got away from the group. I felt sick inside now Mrs McGiven had said I was leaving. It made everything so final.

Now it was clear I had only a few weeks until Easter, and the dreaded move to Wales. Mum didn't seem to want to talk about it, which is unusual for her - she normally wants to talk about everything, all the time. About my homework, her day, my tests at school, friends, everything. And usually she wants to talk when I'm trying to listen to something really good on TV. So it's weird that she didn't want to speak about the single most drastic thing that's ever happened to us; moving away from all our family and friends. I think it may have been my fault - because every single time Wales was mentioned, I piped up, 'Can I have a dog?... When am I getting my dog?'

Davey was spending more and more evenings round at our flat. The first few times he didn't turn up until after I'd gone to bed to watch my TV, but then he began to appear earlier in the evening, and before long he was coming to supper three or four times a week.

It's weird, but when I had Mum all to myself I used to get annoyed with her endless chatting, especially when I was busy. But now I'm longing for an evening together on the sofa, watching an old video or *Who Wants to be a Millionaire?* She's such a good laugh, completely useless with technology, clueless about iPods and music, but clued up about life. She knows most of the answers on *Millionaire*, and she explains the plot of any film when I don't get it. We're a good team, and we don't need anyone else pushing in.

One evening, Mum was serving up Davey's meal in the kitchen while he sat in front of the football with his feet on our coffee table. I am never allowed to put my feet on it. Never.

I was helping wash up the debris from breakfast. Anything to avoid being in the same room as HIM.

'Can I eat supper in my room please?' I asked Mum.

'No you can*not*,' she hissed, 'Don't be so beeping rude, he's a guest.' (She always says 'beeping' when she's a bit annoyed. When she's truly angry she says the actual swearwords. And then she has the cheek to tell me not to swear. She asked me once 'Where do you learn all this foul language?'

And I replied, 'From you.' She didn't appreciate that one bit. Adults don't like you to tell them the truth.)

'Is that OK for you darling?' Mum crooned at Davey as she watched him stuffing his face with our Chicken Kiev.

'Mmm,' he replied, without taking his eyes off the TV screen.

'Did you have a good day?' she tried again, wanting a conversation.

'I'm trying to listen,' he said curtly.

I carried on eating my meal in silence at the table. The table where Mum and I always sit to eat our supper, even though I beg and beg to be allowed to eat it on my knee in front of the telly. Just as slimey Davey was being allowed to do right now.

'Come and join us on the sofa love,' Mum said to me,

smiling a feeble smile, though her eyes looked sad.

'I'm fine here,' I replied. No way was I joining Davey on the sofa. Even though it would put me nearer to the football.

I carried on chewing my chicken, and wanting the evening to be normal, just me and Mum together, like every night used to be.

We sat in silence for the rest of the meal, which gave me time to hatch my plan. A plan to get my own back on Mum and Davey. Some of my ideas were a bit mad, (like running away from home), but I had nowhere to run except Gran-Wen's and I knew she would bring me straight back to Mum. So I considered catching the train into London and living rough with the kids you see outside the cinemas in Leicester Square. But as they do drugs and have even less money than me, I wasn't totally keen - it could be even worse than living with Mum and Slime-man. So I was left with my best idea of all, to steal a dog and keep it hidden from Mum. She had made it perfectly clear that Davey hates dogs, and now he had almost moved in, drastic action would be needed to make sure I got the pet I longed for. A dog was the only thing that would make a move to Wales bearable.

Little did I know how quickly I was going to find myself putting the plan into action.

It all happened by accident in the end. Two weeks before breaking up for Easter and my last day at school, we had a school trip into London for RE. We'd been studying the Muslim faith, and Mrs Bennett had arranged a trip in a coach to visit the Shepherd's Bush mosque. We love school trips. You get most of a day off lessons, someone is bound to be sick on the coach, and we always manage to do something that's totally banned. Some teachers are better than others for school trips - Miss Wallace is rubbish because she keeps us under strict control, especially the boys, but Mrs Bennett is one of the easy ones.

The trip round the mosque was OK, and we all had a bit of a laugh because Stuart Jenkins managed to stand behind Mrs Bennett and pull stupid faces while she was telling us about the Seven Pillars of Islam. He did a chimpanzee (by pulling his ears out and making himself cross-eyed), a pig (pushing his nose up), and a donkey. The 'Hee-haw, Hee-haw' was what gave him away.

Mrs Bennett turned round and yelled at him, 'Try and behave as if you are in a church Stuart Jenkins, instead of a zoo,' as we all stifled our shrieks of laughter.

A man in a long purple robe stared at us from a door in the wall.

After we came out into the bright daylight of a busy Shepherd's Bush, Mrs Bennett thought we had enough time to look round the local street market before returning to our coach. The place reminded me of the setting in *Notting Hill* where Hugh Grant has a bookshop. Lively, busy, crying out to be explored.

'This is a very multi-cultural area and we'll see all sorts of interesting foods and produce. Now keep very close together and don't wander off,' pleaded Mrs Bennett.

I thought that was a bit like asking a bunch of two year olds not to wet their nappies. We're teenage boys - how can we help wandering off?

Stuart Jenkins, Gary Pershore and I stood at the back of the group and waited for our moment. It came while Mrs Bennett had gathered the form around a fruit and veg stall. She was yapping on about lychees, yams and stuff, and the stall-holder was trying to look relaxed about a bunch of teenagers crowding out his customers. Our school helper was picking up bits of jewellery on the next stall. She was in her own little world, turning necklaces over in her hands.

'How many of you have ever tasted okra?' Mrs Bennett asked us.

Then the stall-holder tapped her on the shoulder and beckoned her towards him.

With her back turned, and attention diverted, our chance came. Stuart Jenkins tugged my collar, and we scuttled away into the crowd.

We dashed into the nearest shop which proved to be a pet shop, and tried to look normal, rather than three school-boys on the run. I had a total of £3.50 in my pocket; my lunch and emergency money. Stuart and Gary went off to look at the guinea pigs, birds and fish, but I knew exactly what I wanted to see. The dog stuff. They didn't have any puppies, but there was a display stand of leads, bowls and dog toys. There wasn't much for under £3.50, but after a while I chose a collar. Don't ask me how I knew the right size for my dog Chinks that I'd never met, but I could picture him so clearly. And the tan leather collar would look really good with his brown patches, and show up well against the white fur.

I took it to the till, and stroked the leather with my fingers, imagining how soft Chinks' fur would feel underneath. He would have snuggly ears and shiny black eyes.

'What's that for?' Stuart called.

'My dog.'

'You ain't got a dog.'

'Yet.' I replied.

Stuart went back to the tank of Neon Tetras.

When we came out of the pet shop our form had disappeared. That was a major relief, and we knew exactly where the coach was parked until it was due to leave at 2.15.

Gary checked his watch, 'We've got an hour of freedom,' he grinned.

We wandered down the street looking at the market stalls. I had only 41p left, but Stu and Gary had money on them. Gary wanted to buy a pair of imitation Raybans but at eight pounds he could only dream. Stu bought a packet of gob-stoppers and a really cheap computer game.

'That'll never work,' Gary told him. 'You can see it's a pirate - the cover is a photocopy and the box is second-hand.'

'It'll still be OK,' Stuart argued, 'I've seen it in Smiths for £29.99.'

'Yeah well at least that one would work.'

Gary was looking at the bras and knickers on the next stall. 'Hey - I've got an idea,' he laughed, 'Give us your phone Stu.'

'What for?'

'Just give it here.'

Stuart handed over his Nokia.

Gary picked up a black thong from the stall and put it on my head upside-down and back-to-front so that the strap (decorated with sparkly bits), was over my forehead. Then he took a photo of me with Stu's camera phone.

'Oi, sod off, you little brats,' yelled the fat woman who ran the stall.

I threw the thong back onto the table and we legged it down the street, killing ourselves laughing.

The picture was a classic - the cross-pattern over my forehead made me look like a Viking.

'Shame you can't really tell they're knickers!' said Stu.

'Right, who can we send it to?' Gary asked.

'Your brother, no, I know... try Neil Morrison.'

'He wouldn't even know what a thong was! What about Hayley Adams?'

'Yeah, go on. I've got her number.'

I had stopped listening. Because I had seen a sight that broke my heart. On the ground beside a nearby meat stall was a wooden crate. And in the crate was a small white chicken. A real live one, with a sign on it saying FRESH POULTRY - LOVELY FLAVOUR £4.99.

So they must be selling the bird for someone to kill and eat it. Even though the chicken was bedraggled and small, standing in its own poo, it was gorgeous. Fluffy, sad and gorgeous.

If I didn't act quickly, it would be dead by nightfall, perhaps sitting in somebody's oven as the temperature got hotter. I just couldn't bear the thought.

I turned to the boys, 'How much money have you got between you?'

'Why?'

'Just count your money!'

Stuart picked a few coins out of his pocket, and Gary opened his school purse. I retrieved my 41p and began to total theirs. Stuart had £2.26, Gary just over a pound.

'You shouldn't have bought that dumb pirate game,' I moaned. 'We haven't got enough.'

I pointed at the crate. Both my mates looked shocked.

'That's sick, selling a live chicken,' said Stu.

'Who kills them?' asked Gary.

'No-one's killing that one,' I said, and meant it. 'How much for that chicken?' I called to the Asian lad on the stall.

'Read the sign,' he called back.

'But it's only a small one,' I said, and then had a bit of inspiration. 'Mum wants enough for the whole family.'

'Shouldn't you be at school?' he asked.

'It's lunch break. Can I have it for a pound less?'

'As it's the last one, I'll knock 50p off.'

I did some mental maths, we needed £4.49 and we had £3.72. It wasn't enough. The little chicken was looking down at the ground, not moving at all, except blinking its eyes.

'Stonking!' shouted Stu as he pulled a pound coin out of his school bag, 'I forgot my bus money!'

I handed over the cash proudly. The Asian lad leaned down and opened the wooden cage, and to my horror, he lifted the chicken out by its legs and passed it to me upside down. 'Keep your eye out for the Bill,' he winked.

'Don't I get the cage as well?'

'Are you stupid or what?' he said, thrusting the bird into my hand. It flapped its wings madly and tried to escape. I didn't know what to do, but something inside told me to keep calm. I turned it the right way up, cupped my arm around the body and held the legs underneath firmly with my other hand. Immediately the bird settled, tucking its head down by shortening its neck. It felt so warm and soft in my hands.

'What the heck are you going to do with it now?' asked Stuart.

So I had a live chicken, nothing to carry it in, and a school bus to catch. After which I would have to walk home to our flat. Suddenly this didn't seem such a good idea. But when I looked at the bird's little eyes I felt the rush of sympathy coming back, and vowed I was going to save this chicken, no matter what.

All three of us had our school bags on our backs.

'Can I put my stuff in your bag Stu?' I asked.

'No Joel, no! You can't put a live chicken in your school bag.'

'You got a better idea?'

So Stuart took my bag and removed my lunch box, file and pencil case. 'Yuck - there's dirty socks in here!' he said with disgust.

'The chicken will be all right in the bag,' said Gary, 'cos when you put a blindfold on a hawk it goes still and quiet, like they did in Henry VIII. You know - when they took birds of prey out hunting.'

'Yes, yes,' I said enthusiastically.

But the chicken had other ideas.

Slowly, carefully, I tried to lower the bird into my (almost) empty bag. But as soon as I released my grip from under its body, it began to flap its wings. Which were massive once it stuck them out. And then it flailed its legs as well.

'Hold it, hold it! Stuart yelled.

'I'm trying. Idiot!' I said, attempting to grab it back again into a firm hold.

Once it had calmed down in my arms, I had another go. Same result as the first time.

'So why don't we cover its eyes up, like I said?' asked Gary.

'It might be worth a try,' I agreed.

'Use one of your old socks,' he suggested.

'I'm not picking up one of those rank socks,' said Stuart, folding his arms.

'Don't be stupid, we've got to hurry for the coach,' I said, 'and I'm holding the chicken, so I can't sort out the sock as well.'

Because Gary had the idea about the blindfold, he eventually agreed to stick his hand inside my bag and fish around for the sock.

'Right, now open it and slip it on his head, like a hat,' I ordered.

Gary pulled a face and rolled up my PE sock.

I stroked the bird's head gently and turned it towards Gary.

'He's put his head down, I won't be able to get it on.' Gary said.

'Try,' I said.

The chicken didn't seem too bothered by the sock as it approached. Gary slid it over the beak, then the eyes, and left the rest of the sock piled up on top of the white ball of feathers.

'Is that on?' he asked.

Luckily for us, at that moment the chicken helped by sticking its neck out, and Gary took the chance of pulling the sock further down. Straight away the bird calmed down.

'Perfect!' I said, 'Open the bag.'

This time it was easy. The chicken didn't resist and fitted really snugly at the bottom of my schoolbag.

'Should we leave the sock on his head?' Stuart asked,

peering inside.

'It's a girl, chickens lay eggs so they must be girls,' I said.

'It seems happy anyway,' said Gary.

'But it might not be able to breathe, it'll die of smelly-feet poisoning,' Stuart added.

So on balance we decided to take off the sock and shut the bag quickly so the light wouldn't get in and disturb it.

'What if it moves, or crows while we're on the coach?' Gary asked.

'Pray,' I said. 'Pray it'll keep quiet.'

'Chickens don't crow, that's cockerels,' Stu added.

'It'll have to keep quiet all night as well - or your Mum'll find it.' Gary replied.

We made our way towards the pub car park opposite the mosque. Now we would be in trouble for playing truant AND smuggling livestock on to a DAN ANDERSON LUXURY COACH. Not great timing as we'd just had a rocketing from our Head in assembly about this being Ryton High's very last chance with DAN ANDERSON LUXURY COACHES. During the infamous year 10 trip to the swimming pool, Melanie Sykes had got into a fight with a girl from another school. After the fight, her mates threw stones and bricks at our kids on the DAN ANDERSON LUXURY COACH. Melanie was suspended and our school had to pay for repairs to the coach.

'We are very fortunate that the coach company are giving Ryton High a final chance,' Mr Heelis had barked at us in assembly, 'There are no other firms prepared to carry school parties, and frankly, with behaviour like this, I don't blame them. You have been warned.'

So our trip to the mosque was the trial run on which the future of all school trips would depend. And I didn't think Mr DAN ANDERSON would be too pleased to find a chicken from Ryton High running loose on his luxury coach at this point. My stomach felt knotted up as we approached the car park.

'I've got an idea!' yelled Gary. 'Let's pretend we've been in the pub for a pee. Mrs Bennett will never notice we've been missing.'

So we lurked at the corner of the pub until our group appeared from the direction of the market. We watched Mrs Bennett rounding up the form and taking her clipboard out of her bag. Then she looked around her. We flattened ourselves behind the pub wall.

'Does anyone need the toilet before we leave?' we heard her call.

This was our chance. I peeped round the corner and saw a small group of girls gather round the helper. They came towards the pub.

'Stay out of sight,' I hissed to the boys.

Just as the last pupil went into the pub, we slipped in behind her and joined the group. So by the time we came out, no-one realised we hadn't been there all along.

Mrs Bennett was ticking off names.

She ticked us off too.

'Good job we hadn't been abducted. Or murdered,' Stu whispered, 'She hasn't even noticed we'd disappeared.'

Stuart sat by Gary so I had to sit next to Neil Morrison. Everything went well until we reached the Staines roundabout. The coach was waiting to pull out and Neil suddenly leaned towards me, saying, 'Why's your bag moving?'

'It isn't,' I said firmly.

'It just moved. I saw it. What's in there?' he poked the bag.

'Don't do that.'

'Have you got a pet in there?' he quizzed me. Turning to the seat behind, he said, loudly, 'Joel's got a pet in his bag.'

I looked at Stu and Gary desperately.

Quick as a flash, Gary shouted out 'Miss - Neil Morrison just farted. Tell him Miss.'

The whole coach erupted into hysterics.

'I did not Gary Pershore, I did NOT!' Neil was shouting above the din, but it was no good. The whole coach began chanting, 'Fart! Fart! Fart!' until Mrs Bennett lost her patience. Thankfully the coach was already pulling into the school playground.

'Thanks mate,' I said to Gary as we shoved our way down the aisle.

Then I had a sickening realisation that when I move to Wales I'll be without him and Stu. Things'll be so bad, I'll even miss Neil Morrison.

As I stepped off the coach, I could tell the chicken was getting restless. It seemed to be trying to turn round inside my bag. I guessed she was probably hungry.

'Oh no!' I thought, as I realised the next problem. I didn't have any chicken food, or any money to buy some.

I hung the bag carefully over my shoulder and began the half-mile trudge home. This would give me time to think.

Immediately I had a brainwave, and diverted off my usual route, making for Gran-Wen's house. Gramps always feeds the wild birds, robins and blackbirds - you name it, he feeds it, and I reckoned a chicken could manage on wild birdseed for twenty-four hours until I could buy some proper food.

I hoped their house would be empty, and I had my own key. But Gramps came to the door as soon as I knocked.

'Hello Jo-Jo!' he said, and I ducked, to prevent him slapping me on the back. Or on the chicken.

I left the bag on the front step. 'Can't stop,' I said, 'but can you lend me some bird seed?'

'What for?' Gramps asked. I am always amazed at the stupidity of questions asked by adults.

'To feed the birds.'

'But you don't have a garden.'

I thought quickly, 'We're doing a project about... nature, and I want to start feeding the birds out of my bedroom window.'

'You'll need a feeder then Jo. Why not wait 'til the weekend and I'll take you to the retail park. We can get everything you need then.'

'No. That's no good. I mean, can't I have just a little bit

of seed now?' I said, trying not to let him hear my rising panic, 'I'll put it on the windowsill without a feeder.'

'That'll never work, but you can have a bit if you want to try.'

Gramps went out of the back door to the shed. I followed to make sure he gave me plenty.

'What sort do you want? I've got peanuts, table seed and feeder seed?'

I tried to imagine what chickens would prefer. I thought they are a bit like pigeons and knew I'd seen those in Gramps garden. 'What do pigeons eat?'

'I don't think you'll get a pigeon coming to your window-ledge Jo,' Gramps said. 'Try table seed.'

He tipped a few spoonfuls into a plastic bag.

'Could I have a bit more?' I begged.

'I don't know how many pigeons you're imagining Joel, but don't be disappointed. Do you want a drink before you go?'

'No thanks, I've got loads of homework,' I lied.

'Well let me know how you get on,' he said, '...with the pigeons.'

'Cheerio,' I waved.

Mum would be at work until after five. I took the chicken indoors, and opened the bag on the kitchen floor.

'Phwor,' I said, as a whiff of chicken poo came out. The bird blinked and stretched and asked to get out.

This was my first chance to look at her properly.

'Chicklet!' I said. 'I'm calling you Chicklet.'

She was pure white, with yellow and black eyes that blinked rapidly. She looked very alert and very wary at the same time. She couldn't trust me, and I couldn't trust her.

Yet. She had a pale pink flap of skin running along the top of her head, between her eyes. And another bit under her beak.

Chicklet was still standing in the bag, wearing it like a skirt round her ankles. I fetched newspaper - Mum would appreciate that - and lifted her out. Then I sprinkled a few grains of Gramps' birdseed on the paper. Chicklet ignored the seed completely and walked about on the paper, lifting her feet quite high. After a bit she stopped and scratched her head really fast with the long yellow toes of one foot. I couldn't take my eyes off her. She was so perfectly made, so alive and real.

'There must be something here that you like to eat,' I said, opening the fridge door. I tried a bit of ham. She pecked and flicked that about, but wouldn't swallow it.

Next I tried a broken biscuit. Which she ignored completely.

So I tried to imagine what a wild chicken would eat. But I couldn't think where chickens live wild, whether they live on hills or on trees. I looked on our egg box for help. It said 'Natural free range eggs, from birds with access to grass.'

'But we don't have a garden!' I said in annoyance. In desperation I re-opened the fridge, looking for something that resembled grass. There was some lettuce and watercress; that was green, so I gave a bit to Chicklet.

Instantly, without hesitation, she gobbled up the leaves. I gave her more. She worked her way though a chunk of an iceberg lettuce before she lost interest. Then she pecked up a few grains of seed. First one or two, then several more. I felt so pleased to see her eating, confident that now she had food inside her she would survive the night.

Checking my watch, I saw that Mum would be home in fifteen minutes. I found an old cardboard box with a lid, and lined it with newspaper. After I had put a small dish of water inside I lifted Chicklet carefully into the box. Immediately she stood in the water and kicked it over.

'Oh no!' I said, 'now the box is soaked through!'

She looked up at me and blinked. Then she began to preen, lifting her feathers with her beak, and nibbling in-between. She looked really happy and so sweet that I couldn't be cross with her.

'It's not going to be much of a life for you in that box,' I said apologetically, 'but I guess it's better than being dead.'

The box wouldn't fit under my bed, but did squeeze into my cupboard once I had taken out a ruck of games and clothes. Three minutes before Mum's arrival time, I shut the cupboard, cleaned up the kitchen floor, and flung myself on the sofa as if I'd been watching TV for ages.

I heard the door of the flat click, the usual pause, then, 'Hi Joel, I'm home.' Another pause, then Mum came through from the hall, and just as usual smiled, 'How was your day?'

'Fine.'

'Good trip?'

'Pretty boring.'

'Fancy a juice?' Mum went into the kitchen.

'Joel, why's all this newspaper in the bin?'

I kept quiet. It's often best to keep quiet at first, adults usually lose interest after a while. Unless it's a VERY serious matter. Then keeping quiet won't save you.

Moments later she called, 'Have you been eating salad?'

'Yup.'

'You hate salad.'

Time to keep quiet again.

Moments later I heard the front door open. Davey came into the sitting room. So he must have his own key now. He ignored me completely, strode into the kitchen as if he owned the place, and I heard the sickening sound of adults kissing hello. This was getting worse and worse. If he had a key, it was only a matter of time until he would be living here full-time.

Every so often I went to check Chicklet in my cupboard. Somehow having her there made me feel slightly less dreadful about Davey. I could only take small peeps at her, without letting in too much light, or she became restless and wanted to get out of the box. But her blinky eyes, and soft, soft feathers just helped somehow.

After supper I announced I would watch TV in my room.

Davey called out to me, 'I want a bar of chocolate, go down to the corner shop and get me one.'

'It's dark. Mum doesn't let me go out in the dark.' I replied.

'Well I do let you, so get off your lazy backside and fetch my chocolate.'

'I'll go,' Mum said, lifting her coat off the peg.

'It's all right Mum, I'll do it,' I said.

'We'll go together.'

As we walked down the street, hunched against the wind, I asked her, 'Why didn't you make him go. It's his chocolate?'

'It's just easier this way,' she replied.

'Are you afraid of him?'

'Don't be silly. Course not.'

'Why do you like him? If you need a boyfriend, why does it have to be him?'

'Life isn't that simple. He's having a few problems at the moment, but you'll grow to like him when you know him better. And I need a man in my life, because it's really tough when everyone else is part of a couple. I'm not getting any younger Joel, and you won't be around forever. Davey is the man I need.'

We were only gone a few minutes, but I knew something was wrong the moment we walked through our front door. Davey was standing in the hall with his hands on his hips, looking thunderous and threatening.

He stabbed the air with his finger, 'Is there something you want to tell your mother?'

I stood closer to Mum.

'Whatever's the matter Dave?' she said, moving towards him.

He brushed her away, and grabbed me by the coat.

'Gerroff!' I yelled.

'Dave, stop it, for heaven's sake,' Mum pleaded.

He dragged me into the bedroom, where, to my horror I saw Chicklet's box in the middle of my floor.

'What the sodding hell do you think this is?' he shouted at me.

Mum bent down to open the flap of the box.

'Don't do that Caitlin, it'll peck you. It's already pecked me,' he said.

Mum peeped into the box, 'It's a chicken!' she exclaimed.

'And what's a ruddy chicken doing in our flat?' Davey yelled at me.

'This is not YOUR flat!' I screamed, 'It's my flat, my bedroom and it's MY chicken!'

'You cheeky little ....'

I seized the box, but Davey was stronger and wrenched it from me, then took it into the hall.

'Where are you going? What are you doing?' I screamed at him.

'Taking this stinking bird down to the canal,' he shouted

back.

I burst into tears and grabbed his arm, fighting as he tried to kick me off. Then I bit him on the left hand. Really hard.

Davey yelled, dropped the box and tried to snatch hold of me.

'Just stop it. Stop it NOW!' Mum shouted at Davey in a voice I've never heard her use before. It was real anger.

For a moment we all stood still, then I dived down to check that Chicklet was OK. She was very frightened, all squashed into one corner of her box.

I was still sobbing.

'Right,' Mum shouted, quieter now, but still very angry, 'Leave this to me Dave. Come with me Joel.'

'I'm not leaving him with Chicklet,' I shouted.

'OK, give us a minute please Dave.'

Mum crouched down on the hall floor with me as Davey slunk into the sitting room.

'What on earth is going on Jo-Jo? How long have you had this... thing, and where did you get it?'

I let her hug me as I tried to tell her the story. Some of it, but not all the details, especially the part about our escape from Mrs Bennett. But I did say, 'If I hadn't rescued her, she would have been in somebody's oven by now. Please Mum, you've got to let me keep her, please!'

'How can we keep a live chicken in this tiny flat love? We've got no garden, it would be miserable. And it will stink, Davey's right about that.'

Which just made me feel even worse.

Then the phone rang.

At first nobody moved, and eventually Mum answered, she seemed distracted, confused. It was Gramps on the phone.

Mum told him about Chicklet, then she listened for a while.

I kept on stroking Chicklet's white feathers, trying to calm her down. I reckoned this wasn't turning into the best day of her life.

'Gramps is coming over,' Mum said as she put down the receiver.

I sat in the hall with Chicklet, Davey was watching TV and seemed to have lost all interest in the situation.

When Gramps arrived he came straight to my box and sat beside me on the floor.

'So this is your pigeon is it mate?' he asked, putting his arm round me, which made me feel tearful again.

'Hey Jo-Jo, we can sort this out, don't you worry. We'll make everything right again,' he said.

'I'll put the kettle on,' said Mum, disappearing into the kitchen.

'Don't bother with tea Caitlin,' Gramps called, 'I'll take Joel home with me.' He turned to me again, 'Would you like to stay the night with me and Gran-Wen?' he asked.

'Mmm' I sniffed, 'and with Chicklet.'

And Gramps did sort things out. He took me back to Gran-Wen, who made cocoa while I told them the story of my day at the Shepherd's Bush Mosque. Every now and again Gramps let out a laugh, which he tried to hide. The bit about the fart and the coach journey home made him guffaw out loud.

When I finished the story he said, 'I know just the right place for Chicklet - in our empty rabbit hutch.'

This idea proved to be less mad than it sounded, and once Gramps had laid straw inside the hutch, Chicklet seemed pretty happy with her new home.

'I'll let her out every morning onto the lawn, and we'll put her away in the hutch at night.'

'Do you think she'll lay eggs?' I asked.

'I'm not sure about that, she's a young pullet, bred to be eaten, rather than to lay, but you never know. She'd need to grow a bit anyway, and put some flesh on those bones.'

Once Chicklet was settled for the night, Gran-Wen tucked me into bed in their spare room.

'I hate Davey,' I said to her with feeling.

'Don't worry about him love, you never know what will happen in the end. As I always say - it isn't over 'til the fat lady sings.'

'What isn't over? Who's the fat lady?'

'It's just a way of saying that things might not stay the way they are right now.'

Next morning Gramps burst into my bedroom at seven o'clock. 'Hey mate, I've got a surprise for you.'

He led me downstairs, out of the back door to the chicken hutch. Chicklet was up already, preening herself and looking really cheerful.

And there in the clean straw was one tiny brown egg, still warm to the touch.

'So I guess she likes her new home!' Gramps said, hugging me tight.

Moving day arrived, and although I had a pet chicken, I was still no nearer to having my very own dog. This was the worst day of my life so far. Right up to the night before, I was still hoping Mum would change her mind about Wales. Even while we packed up our stuff I carried on hoping.

But when Gran-Wen and Gramps arrived in a hired van to help us move our furniture, then I knew it was real.

We'd already agreed that Chicklet could come to Wales, because we'd have a garden, and Gramps had packed the hutch in the van with Chicklet and her food. The fact that I'd be able to live with her was the only good thing about moving.

As we filled the van, the adults were chatty and noisy, but I don't think I said a single word. Every time Gramps took something out of my bedroom I felt worse. One by one, square patches of dirt and dust appeared where my furniture had been. An oblong chest-of-drawers shape with deep ridges in the carpet where the feet had stood, a bed-shaped oblong against the opposite wall. There were paperclips, bits of fluff, sweet wrappers and pen-tops round the edges of my carpet. After Gramps had carried out the last box, as I looked at the squillions of bits of blu-tack on my bare walls, and the un-curtained windows, I knew it wasn't my room any more.

Gran-Wen flew round the flat with the vacuum cleaner, and I sat on the wall in front of our building to watch the final depressing stages. It was beginning to drizzle. I couldn't remember a time when I didn't live in these flats, with Gran-Wen round the corner. It may not be Beckingham Palace but it suits me fine. Wales will be full of Welsh people who do Welsh things with other Welsh people. This has to be the worst idea Mum ever had. While we packed I didn't want to be nice to her because I blame her for breaking up the family. She had a perfectly good job at Sainsbury's. I just don't get it.

While we were packing, Davey rang Mum's mobile a couple of times, but I had a big shock when he suddenly drove up our street in his red Peugeot 205. (1989 - how embarrassing is that?) He said he'd come to wave us off. At least that made me keen to get as far away from Staines as possible.

'Can I ride in the van with you?' I asked Gramps.

'Jump up,' he replied. So we led the way while Mum and Gran-Wen prepared to follow in our Fiesta.

Davey looked totally pathetic as he stood by the kerb watching us drive away. Rain was coming down hard now, making his grey hair stick to his forehead. He didn't want to look stupid, so he didn't smile or wave his arm. Just raised his hand then turned away. I was so angry he was there to spoil my last view of the flat. Then I realised I hadn't said goodbye to it.

It's possible I may have sniffed at this point, because Gramps suddenly patted my knee and said, 'Hey mate - everything will be fine.'

I looked out of the window, 'I'm glad he's not coming with us anyway.'

'Me too mate,' Gramps grinned. He knew it was naughty to say that about Mum's boyfriend, and it made us feel bonded. I reckon he doesn't like Davey any more than I do, and that's going to help somehow.

'When's Davey joining you in Wales Jo-Jo?' he asked.

'Dunno.'

'Things have a funny way of working out. He might even

change his mind about leaving Staines at all.'

I looked out of the van window at the familiar landmarks I pass every day. And wondered whether I'd ever see them again.

It wasn't long before we reached places I've never been. We drove on motorways for ages, stopping for petrol and chips at a service station, but then diverted onto normal roads. At first the countryside was the same as home, but after two or three hours we started to see lumpy hills, then massive mountains. The van struggled up roads built far too steeply. I don't know why they can't just make the Welsh roads flatter and straighter. Like they do in Staines. Obviously the Romans never reached this far, they had more sense.

Gramps kept peering between the windscreen wipers saying, 'The scenery here is beautiful - when you can see it!'

The road signs were in Welsh as well as English.

'Can't they speak English?' I asked Gramps.

'They speak both, but the Welsh are very passionate about their language.'

I tried reading out some of the signs. Either the Welsh road builders are dreadful spellers, or they're having a laugh. *'Felin-fach'* wasn't too bad. *'Allt-ma-wr'* was stupid but I could nearly say it, and then we hit *'Cwmbach Llechryd.'* For heaven's sake - don't they understand that words need vowels?

Gramps was killing himself at my pronunciation.

'How can you have a word starting C-W-M?' I screeched.

'Hey look at the next sign!' Gramps joked, *'Llansantffraed Cwmdeuddwr.* Cwm again!'

The rain got heavier and heavier.

After another hour I thought we must be nearly there. Wrong. The further we went, the stronger grew the sinking feeling in my stomach - I realised we were such a long way from home that Gramps and Gran-Wen wouldn't be able to come very often.

'What's up drivers' mate?' Gramps asked.

'When you leave tonight, how long 'til I see you again?' I asked.

'I'm going to come back for a few days while Gran's at work. In a fortnight's time.'

'It's a long way from Staines,' I said flatly.

'What's a couple of hours between Grandad and grandson eh?' he said trying to cheer me up.

But all I could think about was a new school, having no friends, and no Gran-Wen to go home to. How could Mum do this to me?

The road took us through a steep sided valley for a while, and little by little the clouds began to lift. They had been so low we couldn't make anything out, but gradually we began to see sharply rising green slopes on either side of us. There were sheep clinging on, munching wet grass. Some of them had red smears of paint on their bums, others had bright blue marks. They looked as though they'd been playing paint-ball.

'Why do they paint the sheep?' I asked.

'So the farmers can tell their own flock apart, when one animal gets out of a field and wanders off.

Suddenly I saw a waterfall, 'Look Gramps - a waterfall right by the road!' It was gone already.

'The sun's going to come out by the time we reach the lake - just you wait,' he said.

'Lake?' I asked.

'Just you wait,' he repeated.

Gramps was right about the weather. As we headed west for the last few miles, the clouds had thinned and lifted. I could see hills bigger than I've ever known, massive craggy ones. Ahead of us they were highest of all.

'This is Snowdonia,' Gramps said, 'and that's Cadair Idris, one of the highest in Wales. You're going to be under the protection of that mountain. I've always thought God lives on the top of hills, because Moses met Him on one, so remember - the big guy's looking down on you to make sure you're all right.'

I looked up the slopes and hoped Gramps was right, because I was going to need some help out here.

We rounded a couple of sharp bends and Gramps said, 'Mum just flashed her lights behind us. That's your signal to cover your eyes Jo-Jo.'

'Why?'

'Orders are orders. I'm closing mine already.'

I laughed at his joke and covered my eyes, 'Can I open them yet?'

'Not till Mum flashes again. And no peeping.'

The van swayed a bit, then stopped and Gramps said, 'Right. Open them.'

The first thing I noticed was how bright it was, because the sun had come out. And ahead of the van was a lake. I don't know how many lakes you've seen, but forget them all. This was nothing like the boating lake, or the lakes at Center Parcs, or any other lake. Even if I try my best with all the describing words Mrs McGiven ever taught us in English lessons, they wouldn't give you the right picture. Water flat and smooth like a piece of dark glass. Golden-green mountains rising out of the water and up to the sky. And on the surface of the water an upside-down matching mountain was reflected back at the first. Reeds at the water's edge, and a strange, tall bird standing with its shoulders hunched, watching the surface.

'Wow. Wow!' was all I said.

'Wow,' Gramps replied.

Suddenly Mum was banging on the van window. She opened my door and asked, 'Well?'

I felt choked up, she sort of pulled me forward, and we ended up hugging. When Mum let me go, her cheeks were wet.

'Why are you crying Mum?' I asked.

'I'll be fine, we'll be fine.'

We followed the Fiesta this time, as Mum wound along the only road, which sticks close, close to the water's edge. There's nothing but the lake, sheep and mountains. You might think that sounds boring, but it wasn't. I was thinking about water-skiing and mountain-biking and stuff like that. Pity I haven't got a bike.

We passed a hotel, church and a pub, then rounded a bend and the lake disappeared. I wanted to turn the van round and go straight back. But after a mile or so, Mum indicated left up a farm track and we bounced our way towards a group of grey farm buildings.

Mum got out and spoke to a man who pointed further up the lane, then gave Mum a key. We carried on in the direction he had pointed up the stony, bumpy track which now had a green grassy stripe up the middle. Maybe the Welsh can't afford tarmac. It wasn't long before we arrived in front of a terrace of grey stone cottages. There were three front doors, but only the first cottage had windows and a proper door, the others were half way to falling down. I peered through the windscreen at the derelict building, with the middle door off its hinges, grass and thistles up to head height. Surely no-one could live here?

'So this is home!' Mum shouted as she slammed the Fiesta door.

'Well, it's certainly a challenge,' replied Gran-Wen getting out.

Gramps just let out his breath slowly in a low whistle.

'How can we live in a ruin?' I asked.

'That boy's a mind-reader,' Gramps said.

But Mum wasn't having any of it, she unlocked the peeling front door and let us inside.

'Poooo-ee!' I yelled, 'this place stinks!' Because it did.

'It does smell really damp,' Gran-Wen added.

The carpets were thin, torn and filthy. The wallpaper was faded, patterned and peeling. But that was luxury compared to the bathroom. I'll keep this short. Fungus, mould, and poo stains inside the loo. Get the picture? Mum screamed when she saw the poo stains. Gran-Wen just leaned against the doorframe and put her hands in her hair.

Suddenly I noticed Gramps was missing. I went back downstairs and looked up the track - he was just disappearing in the direction of the farm. He was gone a while, long enough for me to explore the garden, the old outside loo, back yards, sheds and wide stream that ran beside the cottage. It babbled and rushed over stones, and was perfect for making a dam. There was nowhere in Staines we could ever make a dam, and I wished Gary and Stuart were here to build one with me. A brown and white bird was dipping into the water from a smooth round stone. When I moved, she flew.

I looked into the sheep field where the sheep watched me as they chewed. They stared at me, and I stared at them. I said 'baa-baa,' a couple of times, but they just stared some more and went on chewing.

Suddenly Gramps called down the track, 'Good news Jo-Jo. Time for a family conference.'

We went indoors and I yelled, 'Mum, Gran!'

The conference was in the kitchen. All our family conferences happen there. We pulled up four filthy chairs. Mum looked as if she'd been in tears while I'd been exploring.

'Righto,' Gramps began, 'I've spoken to Mr Jones, and we've come to a deal.'

'I'm not living here,' Mum butted in.

I stared at her, confused because a few minutes earlier she had seemed quite cheerful about the cottage.

'Well what a shame, because he agreed you could stay here rent-free,' Gramps grinned.

Mum looked up and blinked. She was listening.

'I told Mr Jones this place isn't fit for pigs to rent as a sty, or words to that effect. And I told him that if it was renovated, he could make some serious money out of it, so he agreed you could live here for three months rent-free - as long as you spend your rent money doing it up.'

'Me! I can't do DIY Dad!'

'You can try. Let's get the van unloaded, and I'll find a hardware store.'

Mum refused to have any of our clean furniture in the filthy house, so Gramps stood it all in the lane outside. My bed was on its end, and everything looked awful, as if we were running a car boot sale in the lane.

Next Gramps made us all help him strip things out of the cottage so he could take stuff to the tip.

'Won't Mr Thingy be annoyed if we tip all his stuff? I asked him.

'All part of the deal,' said Gramps. 'This place gives his wife the creeps and he said he'd be glad to see the back of the things.'

'Why does it give her the creeps?'

Gramps bit his lip. I reckoned he was wishing he hadn't told me.

'No idea. But it had the same affect on me when I walked in. Must be the dirt and damp.'

We ripped up all the carpets, emptied the shed, and took down the curtains and lampshades. My hands were black when we finished, even by my usual standards. Then Gramps loaded the van with rubbish and drove off. He said he could be a long time.

Mum made us a cup of tea and sat talking with Gran-Wen in the sunshine, Gran was pulling up weeds from where she sat, just like she does in her own garden after Sunday lunch.

I dipped in and out of their chatter, not really listening; 'I can't stay Caitlin, but your Dad could drop me at the station and I'll get back in time for work.......How long could he stay?..... How cheaply can you refit a kitchen?'

As soon as they'd finished tea, Mum and Gran-Wen began the decontamination process indoors. When I saw the rubber gloves and bottles of bleach, I scarpered.

I explored to find the best place for Chicklet, and decided on the little patch of grass at the back of our building. It wouldn't be too difficult to clear the old farm tools and wood to make enough space for her hutch. I wouldn't be able to let her out yet, until Gramps had made some kind of fence, but at least I could put fresh grass in her hutch.

Very carefully, I moved her hutch to her new home. She seemed to like the Welsh grass I pushed through her door. I was so glad to have her, although she's not as good as a dog, at least she's mine. And she lays an egg nearly every day, a small deep brown one with a rich golden yolk.

If you came out of the cottage and turned left you reached the gate of the staring sheep. If you turned right you went back to the farm. I turned right. And didn't get far before I had a shock.

Out of nowhere I heard a voice in a very strong accent yelling, 'Stuff off. We don't want you here.'

I turned and ran back towards the cottage.

'Coward!'

So I stopped and pretended I was looking at the stream. Picked up a twig and dropped it in, wishing I could work out where the voice was coming from.

'English coward!'

There was no-one either left or right down the lane. So I looked up. Sitting above me in a big tree was a person who seemed to be a girl. I could just make out a dark boiler suit and a mass of red curly hair.

If it was only a girl, I wasn't scared. It occurred to me that if I sat at the foot of the tree, she couldn't get down. That would annoy her more than me shouting up an insult. So it's what I did. Sat against the trunk and took my game-boy out of my pocket. I'd found it when we cleared my bedroom, and it still worked. Before long I forgot all about the kid in the tree.

'Oi!' she shouted.

I carried on playing snake.

'You deaf? Move!'

This was the highest score I'd ever had.

'Ouch! You idiot!' I yelled, as she landed on my shoulders and crushed me to the ground.

'In my way, you was,' she said, in the same thick, but soft accent. The last word went up at the end, as if the sentence were a question. Weird. The way I would say, 'Surely you don't support Man United?' Making the last word the most important.

She stood right in front of me and I could see she was much younger than me. I'm fourteen, and she looked eight. Ish.

'What's that?' she pointed at the game-boy.

'It's mine, that's what.'

'Whass your name?'

'Joel.' I carried on with snake.

'Aren't you wanting to know my name?'

'Not really.'

'It's Siriol.'

I looked up. 'Cereal? Is that your nickname? Like Weetabix?'

'No, idiot. Siriol. It's Welsh. Meaning cheerful, bright.' The way she said it was very soft, like a purr.

'Better than Weetabix!' I smiled. 'How old are you?'

'Thirteen.'

'Liar!'

'I am as well, ask my Da?' Even in anger her voice was soft.

'Thirteen next month.'

'So you're twelve then. You're very short for a twelve year old.'

'We don't eat so much junk food in Wales as you *Eng*lish.' Up at the end again, just like a question.

She tried to grab my game-boy.

'Hey,' I yelled and pulled her arm. Siriol was tough as any boy. Most girls would have giggled and let go, but she held on and rolled over on the lane in a fight. It was fun, even though I was much stronger.

'Siriol!' called a deep voice.

We let go of each other. Siriol turned her mass of red hair up the lane towards the farm.

'Coming Da! I've gotta go,' she said. 'See you *la*ter.'

'See you.' I began a new game of snake.

Suddenly she stuck her head down between my face and the game-boy and asked, 'Do you like dogs?'

How did she know? Why did she ask that? I stared intently at her pale eyes and small mouth, the froth of ginger curls falling around and in front.

'Because if you want a dog, I can get you one.' And she ran home, swift as a dart.

I was still in shock when Gramps returned in the van. Round and round in my head went Siriol's words. She could find me a dog. A dog. My dog.

This wasn't the right time to announce it to Mum. I could just tell.

The hired van was full. Gramps had bought wood, tiles, flat-pack kitchen units. Curtain poles, flooring and rugs.

Mum hugged him, 'Dad! You must have spent a fortune!'

'Call it an early wedding present!' Gramps replied, putting his arm around her shoulder. I definitely didn't like the sound of that.

Best of all, he had a huge parcel of fish and chips from Tywyn. We ate them on the front porch and nothing ever tasted so good. I hadn't realised my stomach was completely starving.

'Change of plan Joel,' Mum said, dipping a chip into her tiny square carton of sauce. 'Gramps is going to stay for a few days, but Gran-Wen will go home on the train.'

'I've run out of tomato ketchup.'

Mum passed me hers, 'We'll get the basics straight before Gramps leaves.'

'Where are we sleeping tonight?' I asked.

'I'll put your mattress in the van,' Gramps said.

Suddenly Mum threw her head back and laughed, 'It's so awful that it's funny,' she said. 'Here we are, eating chips in the back of beyond, and my new home's so bad I can't bring the furniture in!' She laughed again.

As she was happy, this was a good moment to make my announcement, 'I'm getting a dog from a girl called Siriol.'

All three adults looked at me hard, but before anyone could answer we heard the peep-peep of a car horn. Round the bend in the lane sped an old red Peugeot. I would have known it anywhere.

'Davey! Mum leapt up and raced to the car, throwing open the driver's door and wrapping herself round Dave's ugly body.

I put my head in my hands, saying, 'Oh no!'

Gramps stood up, and Gran-Wen pulled me towards her in a hug.

'No, please no,' I was whispering under my breath.

Dave got out and surveyed us sneeringly. 'Nice place,' he said sarcastically.

Mum was still draped around his neck, 'So you left. You've left her. Oh Davey!'

He unclasped her arms roughly and sauntered up to the cottage, 'I assume we're not staying?'

'Oh but we are, Dad has sorted everything out and we've got it rent-free,' Mum said in a pleading sort of way.

Gramps moved towards Dave, 'Good timing mate, you'll be able to help me.'

'I've got plenty of experience,' Dave boasted, 'I pretty much built my sister's place in Cornwall. Plastering, brick-laying, done the lot.' And he was off, droning on about himself, his talents, and how brilliant he is. I knew Gramps wouldn't have another chance to speak.

At that moment I hated Mum, felt so angry with her. Only a few minutes earlier we'd been happy, and I was starting to believe we could live here, that Wales might be OK, and I was 99% sure I was having a dog. Now the step-dad from hell has turned up and ruined everything.

The sky was streaked with dark by the time Gramps put Gran-Wen in the van and set off for the train station. Losing her was the last straw for me. The thought of staying in the cottage with Mum and HIM was just too much, so I ambled up the lane towards the farm, hoping I might see Siriol to ask her about the dog.

Once my eyes got used to being outside, the sky appeared lighter and I could see my way along the track pretty easily. To be honest the farmhouse isn't in a much better state than our cottage, it's less ramshackle, but messy with churns and tools and old tractors outside. I wasn't sure which was the best door to knock on, but chose the front as I didn't like the look of the mad dog on a chain round the side.

The amount of leaves and dead moths in the porch made me realise the ginger-haired girl and her family don't use this entrance much.

I knocked once quietly.

Nothing.

Again, louder.

Nothing.

Again, really loudly.

'I'm watchin' the telly.'

I backed out of the porch and looked up to see where the voice was coming from.

A ginger-framed white face was peering down from an upstairs casement. (That's the word for an old window - like a Tudor one. This was definitely a casement.)

'Oh's you,' Siriol said in her kind of Welsh purr, 'Come round the back.'

'There's a dog.'

'I thought you liked dogs.' She slammed the window.

There was nothing for it, my only chance of watching

Eastenders was to walk past the mad chained-up dog in the dark.

As soon as I approached, the dog jumped to the end of its chain and started to bark crazily. Pulling, straining and barking loud enough to wake the dead. I hoped the chain would hold.

A chink of light framed the back door and I made a dash for it, pushed the door open and stepped into what turned out to be a kitchen. The sort of room where you'd expect to find a fat cook in an apron - just as we did on the Acton Wold trip in year 4. This kitchen was the same - with an old-fashioned range cooker, a square white sink, and a slatted rack hanging above the enormous kitchen table. This is where the fat cook would make mince pies and bread and stuff. At Acton Wold we got to taste her bread.

But there was no-one here except a sleepy cat in front of the range on an old blanket.

I didn't like to go any further, as it felt rude, so I stood for a while, waiting. In a moment the back door flew open.

A man came into the kitchen, a man about Mum's age, with curly red hair like Siriol's but cut shorter.

'Hello then,' he said, making the word 'then' go up at the end, just like Siriol does. It seems to be how you speak Welsh.

'Um, hello,' I said quietly.

'Everything OK at the cottage?'

'Fine thanks.'

'Not what your Granda said!' and he laughed at me, but kindly.

'If it's Siriol you're wanting, she's upstairs,' he said. 'I'll fetch you a cocoa.'

He seemed to think I knew the plan of the farmhouse

intimately. So after it was obvious he wasn't planning to show me the way, I set off on my own. Through a large Acton-Wold-style dining room where a huge grandfather clock slowly ticked, into a Tudor hall with one of those wooden benches with a back called a settle. (At Acton Wold they told us if you were engaged to a girl in Tudor times, you had to sit in a settle by the fire and snog each other. Am I glad I'm not a Tudor teenager?)

The final door downstairs was ajar. I pushed it open gingerly and found a sitting room, with high-backed armchairs, dark furniture, but no TV. The room smelled cold, and didn't look much used.

The staircase was steep, narrow and turned back on itself when you reached halfway. I climbed it, peering through each doorway as I passed. Siriol wasn't in the bathroom, the big dark bedroom, the small damp bedroom, or the office. Then I heard the closing music of *Eastenders* coming from a door ahead of me, at the end of a short corridor. The light was on, so I knocked and pushed the door ajar.

Inside the snug room, Siriol was perched on an old sofa, feet tucked up under her hips, and hugging her knees. She didn't look at me but spoke as if I'd been in the farmhouse a million times before, 'That episode was **rub**bish.'

I was looking round the room for signs of a bed. It seemed weird to have a sofa in an upstairs room.

'Is this your bedroom?'

'No **stu**ped, it's the TV room.'

'Oh.'

'I saw your Da arriving in the red car,' she said.

'He's not my Dad.'

'Well who then?'

'My Mum's..... boyfriend.'

'I'm glad my Da doesn't have a girlfriend.'

'Where's your Mum?'

'She's in the village. Visiting my uncle. He's dying of **can**cer.'

I didn't know the best way of replying to that. 'Oh dear,' I said.

'She goes there every night to cook his tea and wash his pants.'

'I see. Does he only wear pants?'

'No, **stu**ped. If that's your Mam's boyfriend, where's your Da then?'

'I haven't got one.'

'Of course you have a Da.'

'Well I don't, and he's not dead, or divorced, or anything.'

'If you don't have a Da then your Mam must have made a baby in a test tube. Same as that sheep I saw on the telly. It's called Dolly the sheep and the farmer made her out of bits of dead sheep. I saw a doctor on the news who knows how to make new babies out of bits out of a dead baby. So if you get run over, your Mam can pick up some of the bits of squashed skin and take it down to casualty and they can make another version of you. They've only just learned how to do it and it's called clowning.'

'What are you on about?'

'Clowning. If I got run over my Mam wouldn't do that 'cos she doesn't want another baby made out of bits of me, she just wants the real me.' Siriol didn't look too sure about this, but she carried on babbling, 'Well if you haven't got a Da then your Mam must have made you in a test tube, because it's the only way of making a baby unless you've got a man's you know.....'

She paused, and I carried on staring at her as if I hadn't

got a clue.

Siriol pointed at my trousers.

I wanted to make her say it. To make her feel as stupid as I felt. So I said, 'Unless you've got a what?'

She put her hand over her mouth, and pointed at my flies again. 'A thingy.'

'A what?' I pulled a face that said - *I don't know what the heck you mean?*

'You're **stu**ped. A willy **stu**ped.'

At first there was complete silence in the TV room. Then she began to giggle and I couldn't help giggling back. Siriol swung forward from her crouched position and lunged at my legs, pushing me over. I grabbed her leg sharply and she fell over too.

That's when her Dad came in with two mugs of steamy cocoa.

'Glad to see you two are getting on,' he said simply, as if it's the most normal thing in the world for two kids who've just met to be rolling round on the floor fighting. Maybe it happens all the time in Wales.

There was nothing good on the telly. After a while I heard a van going past in the lane outside.

'Your Granda's back,' Siriol said.

'Nosey aren't you?'

'Ob**ser**vant. That's what I am.'

'I'd better go.' I knew I had to ask about the dog before I left - that was the whole reason for my visit, 'You know earlier you said you could get me a dog?' I asked her.

'Might do.'

'What did you mean?'

She paused, tilted her small white face to the side and looked at me sharply, 'That's for me to know and you to find out.'

'You're so..... annoying,' I said, turning away.

'The problem with you *Eng*lish is you can't take a joke,' she giggled. 'Come back Saturday about the dog.'

The two days until Saturday crawled by. All the adults were working on the cottage, doing DIY, and getting tired and aggressive. And I found out you can get sick of looking at staring sheep, they're not much company. You can't take a sheep for a walk, or sit on your bed with it. My choice was - hang around in the cottage and get moaned at by Mum for being in the way, or hang around in the lane. No TV, no friends, none of my stuff. I even started to miss school. How sad is that?

I did find a whole crowd of chickens that hang around Siriol's farmhouse. I counted fifteen, but there may be more, because they move around and it's difficult to count them accurately. They lay their eggs all over the place, in the barns and sheds, and I've no idea where they sleep. There are black ones, brown ones, and some grey and white ones. But they don't have a pure white one like Chicklet. I wondered whether she would get on OK with Siriol's hens, because she seemed miserable in her hutch. I let her out on the grass now and again, but only for short spells in case she wandered off.

It didn't take long for Davey-baby to show his true colours. I'd already started to call him that, quietly under my breath, but he'd heard, and he didn't like it.

If Gramps hadn't been with us I'd have gone completely bonkers in those two days – he started using the name 'Davey-baby' when we were on our own. But he didn't see the worst incident so far with the step-dad from hell.

It happened when I was unbelievably bored on Friday evening, so bored that I took one of Mum's tennis rackets outside, and I was practising my forehand against the side wall of the cottage. My record so far was twelve hits in a row, without missing the ball. I could have done more if there wasn't an old greenhouse on one side which I had to be careful not to smash. Just as I was about to hit number thirteen, Davey-baby came out of the cottage and laughed. One of those sarcastic 'huh-huh' laughs I'm getting to know so well. I dropped the ball immediately.

'Well you're pretty useless,' he jeered, 'even for a kid.'

And it's true - I am pretty useless, at sport and most things. Except swimming, I'm really good at swimming, which isn't much use on the footie field, or in PE. We didn't have anywhere to play outside in Staines, and I never had much practice at sport.

I couldn't even think of anything clever to say back.

Davey went on, 'Useless, small, pathetic…. that's what you are.' Then he kicked Chicklet's hutch and went inside.

I crouched down beside the hutch and wished. Wished Davey would drop dead. Wished he had been in Sri Lanka when the tsunami hit, or that he would get involved in a terrorist plot. Until I met him I didn't know what hate felt like. And I can't understand what Mum is doing with him. All step-parents are difficult, Peter Pike has no end of bother with his step-mum, but Davey is evil. Ugly, orange and evil.

'Lo.'

I looked up and was really glad to see Siriol's red mop of hair.

'Hi.'

'You all right?'

''Mmm.'

'I can tell you're not OK. Don't you like it here?'

'It's fine.'

'This your chicken?' she asked, crouching down beside

me.

'Mmm. It's Chicklet.'

'You should let her out of that hutch.'

'She might escape.'

Without asking, Siriol opened the hutch and made cheeping noises at Chicklet. She lifted her out, pulled open her wings and said, 'We need to clip these.'

'You what?'

'Her wings. Unless we sort these, she can fly up into the trees.' And she set off, with Chicklet under her arm in the direction of the farm.

I followed saying, 'What are you doing?'

'Wait and see, *Eng*lish boy,' she said, smiling in her cheeky way.

At the farm I followed her into an old shed. Still holding Chicklet under her arm, she ferreted about until she found a pair of small shears.

'What the heck are you doing?' I yelled, trying to grab Chicklet.

'Look English, what I don't know about birds isn't worth *know*in. This bird needs her wings clipped.'

'You can't cut her wings off!' I shouted.

'Just shut up, you'll scare her, I'm not cutting off her wings. See here,' she said, extending Chicklet's right wing, 'These last feathers, the long ones, are the primary feathers. A bird needs them to fly. I'm cutting off the last two so she can't fly away. One wing will be longer than the other, and she'll lose her flying balance.'

'Will it hurt?'

'Does it hurt when you cut your hair?'

'Depends on the hairdresser.'

Siriol made quick, expert movements with the shears,

and clipped away the two largest feathers on the end of Chicklet's wing.

'Done!' she said, setting Chicklet on the ground.

She opened the shed door and my hen extended her wings and shook herself. She seemed perfectly happy. Little by little she moved towards the open doorway, then out into the yard. A few of Siriol's hens were pecking the ground outside. A couple of pure white doves flew up from the yard and circled in the air before settling in the eaves of the open barn opposite us.

'I'm a bit worried about her actually,' I said. 'When I first had her, the flappy bit of skin on her head was pale pink, and now it's bright red. Do you think there's something wrong?'

Siriol put her head on one side and grinned at me. 'No, *stu*ped. That's the comb, and it's s'posed to be bright red. The sign of an unhealthy chicken is when the comb goes pale - if it's nearly white then the hen is nearly dead. So you must be doing *some*thin right.'

I felt a rush of relief. Siriol was right, she does know a lot about hens. We stood and watched Chicklet, and almost immediately one of the large brown chickens came over and tried to peck her.

'Oh no!' I yelped.

'S'all right, leave her a minute.'

We waited and watched Siriol's hens as they came nearer and checked Chicklet out. A couple more tried to peck her, and I was really proud when she pecked right back. After a few moments she felt relaxed enough to forage in the yard for grain and bits, just like the other birds.

'She'll be fine, just leave the hutch open, and she'll go back if she wants to.'

'I'm not giving her to you,' I said, worrying that Chicklet

might not be mine any more.

'Whatever. See ya tomorrow Townie-boy.'

'Siriol?' I asked hesitantly.

'What?'

'How did you know I wanted a dog. When you first saw me?'

She looked thoughtful, '*Ob*vious. You looked like something was missing. And I knew it was a dog. See ya.'

'Bye.'

I walked the few metres home with my hands in my pockets and a heavy heart. Chicklet is the only thing that makes me happy here, and I felt as though I had lost her. I left the door of her hutch open and went indoors.

That night I was restless and kept waking up. At first light I crept downstairs and out of the kitchen door to see if I could find Chicklet. The sky was still dark, streaked with pale blue at the edges, and I took my torch. The cockerel started crowing from the direction of the farmyard.

What if Chicklet had been pecked to death in the night by the other hens, or killed by a fox?

I shone my torch into her hutch hopelessly, and had the shock of my life when my flashlight reflected on the pure white of Chicklet's feathers, and beside her one of Siriol's small black and white hens. It was snuggled up to Chicklet as if they'd been reared together, two friendly hens looking at me and blinking into my torchlight.

'Wicked!' I said.

So it looks like things are turning out okay for Chicklet in Wales.

How long are you staying?' I asked Gramps as we ate our Saturday porridge in the scabby, but-no-longer-stinky kitchen. Mum and Davey-baby were still in bed.

'Til the end of the week,' Gramps replied, 'It'll take me that long to do the basics. Davey-baby has offered to help, and he seems pretty handy, so if we can sort the bathroom and kitchen by Friday then I'll go home to Gran-Wen.'

'Can I come back with you for the weekend? Please?'

Gramps looked thoughtful, 'I don't think that would help Jo-Jo. If you went back to Staines so soon, it would make you even more unsettled, and make it harder to come home again. But I promise Gran and I will be here in a few weeks time, and you've got school to look forward to on Monday.'

School! I had completely forgotten about that part of the move. For the last few days it had felt as though I'd left school forever. Now Gramps had reminded me, I realised this was just an Easter holiday, not the end of my education.

Gramps must have seen the horror on my face, 'It'll be OK mate, and you'll pick up the language in no time.'

'What language?'

He paused, 'Didn't you know? They speak Welsh in the schools round here. Welsh and English, but mostly Welsh.'

'But I can't speak Welsh!' I spluttered.

'That nice new friend of yours will help, and at your age you'll pick it up right away.'

I admit, I felt like crying. This was the final blow. Moving to a derelict cottage, Davey, and finally a school where people speak a foreign language. Suddenly I didn't want any more breakfast, and my spoon sank into my porridge. For the first time in my fourteen years, Gramps didn't seem to have anything to say.

In my head I quietly did something I've never done in my life, I said a prayer. I wasn't at all sure how you do one, as I've never been in church, but I closed my eyes and thought the words, 'Dear God, if you're up there on the mountain, please could you help me. Please. Amen.'

Nothing happened, and I didn't feel any different.

'Can I come in?' called a familiar voice from the lane.

'Hello little lady!' Gramps said, opening the door, 'You're just in time for some porridge.'

'My favourite!' she said, pulling up a chair. Siriol is different from anyone I've met, she seems to belong straight away.

'Annie!' Gramps said suddenly, patting her on the shoulder, 'That's who you remind me of!'

Siriol and I both looked blank.

'Have you seen the musical called Annie? There's a film version, she's a red-haired American orphan and she looks just like you.'

'I'm not an orphan,' Siriol said crossly.

'You've got the red hair, big personality, freckles and a smile you can't help falling for,' Gramps went on. You're just the ticket.' He turned to the stove to pour out porridge, 'Just the ticket.'

Siriol pulled a face at me that said 'Is he a nutter?' and we grinned at each other.

She said, 'Well as today is Saturday, we'll be going to find you a dog.'

My heart leaped inside me.

'What's Welsh for dog?' Gramps asked Siriol, looking at me with a sideways glance.

'It's *ci*. And *ci bach* is a puppy,' Siriol replied.

'That's a bit weird, cos I'm calling my dog Chinks, and that's a bit like Ci,' I said.

'Chinks is *tincian* in Welsh.'

'That sounds nice, tin-ki-an,' I said pronouncing it slowly.

'It means tinkle as well as chink, you know like two bits of glass tinkling, chinking together,' she explained.

'Yes, or like two rocks chinking together,' I said.

'You what?'

'Doesn't matter,' I said.

'One more question little lady,' Gramps interrupted. 'What's the Welsh for Grandad? Grandpa?'

'We say *taid*.'

'Tide! I'd like you to call me that little lady. It'll help Joel with learning Welsh.'

'OK you can be my Taid, that's cool. Come on Joel. See you Taid.'

'Where are you off to?' Gramps called after us, 'Mum's bound to ask. And when will you be back?'

'To Abergynolwyn to see my Uncle who's got cancer. About two hours.'

'I thought we were going to see about my dog,' I said as I jogged to keep up with Siriol.

'We ARE going to see about a dog **stu**ped. My Uncle **Gwen**nol is a vet.'

She led me to one of the farm buildings where a couple of old bikes leaned against a bale of straw.

'Are we going to cycle? On those?'

'Is that a **prob**lem townie-boy?'

'Look, stop calling me English, stupid, and townie-boy. You're really getting on my nerves. My name is Joel.'

Siriol looked at me seriously.

'OK,' she said.

The bikes were truly sad. Mine was red, rusty and if I'd been seen on it in Staines, I wouldn't have lived long - the embarrassment would have killed me. But I figured we weren't going to meet many people out here in the wilderness.

'How far is it to Aber-thingy.'

'Abergynolwyn. A couple of miles, it's only a village, and an easy ride, even for a town..... sorry Joel.'

'Does your uncle have pets at his house?'

'Wait and see.'

Siriol cycles as fast as any boy. Her bike is old and heavy but she goes like the wind. I had real trouble keeping up with her, but I don't think she guessed. We went through the village, a small cluster of grey houses, and were soon out of it again. When we had been pedalling for a few more minutes, I heard the sharp, piercing sound of a loud whistle.

'Whass that?' I yelled to Siriol who was a few metres ahead.

'The 10.15!' she shouted back.

Suddenly I saw a massive jet of steam rising through the trees to our left. Between the leaves I caught a glimpse of movement, and then breaking through the cover into full view, a bright red tank engine, pulling one, two, three, four smart brown coaches. From the chimney a puff of steam billowed, and each time the engine chuffed, a new ball of steam came out of the funnel.

The smell was new to me, a sweet sharp smoke scent, and I breathed it in deeply, a smell that said Christmas and long ago. My heart was pumping faster than usual, in time with the thumping heartbeat of the little engine as she accelerated away from us.

'Wow!' was all I said.

'It's Douglas,' Siriol said matter-of-factly, she had dropped back to be level with me.

'You know the driver?'

'Douglas is the name of the engine. Let's race the train!' and she pedalled feverishly along the road. I soon fell behind, but Siriol managed to keep pace with Douglas for a few hundred metres. When I knew I couldn't catch them, I stopped beside the verge and just watched Douglas' funnel and the billow of steam threading through the mountain trees.

When she returned to me, Siriol's forehead was beaded with sweat and she couldn't breathe enough to speak. But in moments she recovered, and we pedalled slowly back to Aber..Aber...Aber-gyn-ol-wyn. Got it!

'Douglas is famous in a way,' she said, rubbing her wet fringe with the arm of her fleece, 'He's in the *Thomas the Tank Engine* books. The bloke who wrote them called him Duncan, he's in *Gallant Old Engine*.'

'I've got that one! I've got all the books!'

'Ooooh is Mummy going to read you Thomas when you go to bed tonight!'

I swerved my front wheel against hers and bashed her on the arm, making Siriol shriek with laughter and swoop away. We played bike tag all the way back to the village and an oncoming car hooted at us angrily.

Without warning, Siriol suddenly pulled into a house drive, and dropped her bike right where she stood, leaving the back wheel spinning in the air. I hung back while she knocked on the door and stepped inside.

'Hey Uncle!' she called, using the front door sill to twist off her wellington boots and flicking away one, then the other. After a moment, I stepped over her abandoned boots, entered the hall gingerly, and left my trainers on the mat. There was no sign of Siriol.

This was the second time I'd had to enter a strange house looking for that girl.

'Come in Joel!' a man's voice called from the front room.

I've never seen anyone with cancer and didn't know what to expect. But I needn't have worried. Siriol's Uncle Gwennol was sitting on an office chair drinking from a mug, and he looked perfectly normal. His front room seemed to be a bedroom and office mixed into one. There was a single bed along one wall, shelves full of big thick textbooks, a good quality sound system and a desk.

Siriol burst out, 'Joel's seen Douglas, and we raced him and Joel couldn't keep up, and he's got all the *Thomas the Tank Engine* books, he's from London and he hasn't got a Da, and his Mam has a boyfriend.'

'Gracious, what an introduction! We hardly need to meet now do we Joel, I know your whole story,' he said, stepping off the chair and holding out his big hand. He lifted mine and shook it firmly and warmly, as if I were grown up.

'I'm Gwennol, and this little monkey's my sister's child,' he said, patting Siriol's hair. 'She's the bane of my life, but if she likes you, she'll be your fiercest friend - no-one messes with Siriol!'

'Have you got any unwanted pets at the moment?' she looked up at him pleadingly, 'and can I sit in your special chair?'

Uncle Gwennol stood up and took sips from his mug, while Siriol jumped into his office chair and swung round and round as if she was riding on a turntable, 'Wheeeeee, wheeee.... do you want a go Joel?'

'What you brings you to God's own country young man?' Gwennol asked me as we watched Siriol whizzing.

'Mum and her.... boyfriend, have come here to set up in business,' I replied.

'What kind of business is that?'

'Selling some sort of creams and make-up with aloe vera in it. The video says you get rich and all your dreams come true and stuff, but I don't think my Mum will.'

'Mmm, and she's come all the way from London for this?'

'From Staines, near London,' I explained.

'I don't think there's much call for that sort of thing around here. For a start there are more sheep than people. And they don't use much make-up.'

I smiled, 'Yeah, I noticed. Are you a sheep vet?'

'I trained in small animals, which means pets, but I work with large animals too, which means mostly sheep in Wales,' he laughed. 'But I'm not too well at the moment, as Siriol may have said. I still work part-time, and I've employed another vet to help me out. As for your other question young lady,' he said, putting his hand on Siriol's shoulder and bringing her to an abrupt halt, 'Why do you want a pet? You've got plenty of animals at the farm.'

'Not any old pet. Joel's dog. It's brown and white and has black eyes. Called Tincian.'

'Oh, you've lost your dog, I'm sorry Joel, we'll keep an eye out for it. What's the breed?'

'One of those,' Siriol said, pointing at a BREEDS OF DOMESTIC DOG chart on Gwennol's wall. 'That's the one.'

I peered more closely at the photograph of a small tan and white dog with a short tail and perky ears. She was right, that was Chinks.

'A Jack Russell Terrier,' Gwennol said, 'OK, tan and white. I'll spread the word.'

I pulled a face at Siriol and raised my eyebrows. I was

waiting for her to tell Gwennol that he had misunderstood, that I haven't actually lost Chinks, it's just that I haven't found him yet. But Siriol didn't say another word about it, and after a few seconds had passed, I didn't like to say anything either.

'Can I show Joel round the kennels?' she asked.

'Of course. And maybe I could have a word with your Mum and ...'

'Davey,' I prompted, looking down at the floor as I said the hateful name.

'Ah, I see – Davey - about the aloe vera business. Maybe I could put them in touch with a few people. Hope to see you again Joel, and I won't forget Tincian, I'll make sure the word goes round.'

As Siriol led me through the back of the house I pushed her from behind, 'Why did you let him think I've lost Chinks? That's a lie.'

'Do you want a dog or not?' she replied crossly. 'And I didn't lie, he just got the wrong end of the stick. The kennels are through here.'

Instead of a garden, the back door of Gwennol's house led into a lean-to, lined on both sides with several animal cages, three high. Large ones at the bottom, the smallest on top.

'There aren't many animals in at the moment,' Siriol explained, 'Hello Buster,' and she leaned down to one of the large cages at floor level. 'He's a collie, belongs to a man who farms beside the lake. But this is Snowy, she's a pet.'

She opened a smaller cage and lifted out a fluffy white terrier.

'She's sweet,' I said, stroking her fur, which was yellowish rather than truly white when you got close, 'But she's not as nice as Chinks.'

'We'll find him,' Siriol said.

My first day at Welsh school came round far too quickly. But what happened on the Sunday night put the thought of school right out of my mind. The weekend had been vile because Gramps had left on Friday to go back to Gran-Wen, and the cottage was cruel and empty without him. I just didn't know how I was going to survive living alone with Mum and Davey-baby.

Although the men had done their best, the cottage now had half a bathroom, and half a kitchen, no carpets, and no heating except one electric fire in the sitting room and the kitchen Aga.

I have a tiny bedroom at the back of the cottage, looking into the side of a hill, and it's completely freezing. I sleep in my sleeping bag underneath the duvet, and still feel cold, even though it's meant to be spring.

And my TV doesn't receive a picture because there's no aerial socket, and although the English are able to make portable TV signals work, the Welsh don't seem able to manage it. So I have to read to send myself to sleep, which makes my arms hurt as I try to hold a book and torch under the heavy bedding. The other night I felt so upset I even read *Gallant Old Engine* about Duncan to try and console myself.

On Sunday I'd gone to bed really early to avoid Davey, and was lying in bed dreading my first day at school, worrying about whether I would miss the bus that's supposed to stop at the end of our farm track, and worrying that the Welsh boys will hate me.

Suddenly I heard yelling from downstairs.

'My private life is my business. She's my wife for God's

sake.' It was Davey.

I couldn't hear Mum's reply. But after a few seconds Davey yelled at the top of his voice, 'I've had ENOUGH!'

Then I heard Mum scream and there was the sound of a piece of furniture being thrown.

I leaped out of bed and rushed to the top of the stairs where I crouched in a position that gave a partial view through the banisters into the lounge.

Mum was sitting on the sofa in tears. In the other corner of the room was one of our dining chairs, lying on its side. Davey was nowhere to be seen.

I crept down a couple of stairs silently. Now I could see him, standing in the kitchen doorway, dialling on his mobile.

'Stupid ruddy network! Hello, Hello... Kelly? It's me. Yes, I'm coming back.'

There was a pause while Davey listened to the voice at the other end.

'I'm coming home...... I'll set off in a few minutes when I've put my stuff together.'

'Yeah, we all make mistakes. Love you, Bye.'

Mum wailed, as if she were in pain, but I was too scared to go downstairs.

I got out of the way just in time as Davey bounded up the stairs, and I could hear him zipping and unzipping bags in the next bedroom. Mum was still sobbing.

After only a few minutes I heard him thunder down the staircase again, and the kitchen door banged.

'Don't leave me!' Mum cried out, but already his car was accelerating away down the lane.

An awful silence descended on the cottage, and I felt completely helpless. I crept down to Mum slowly and quietly, wishing I wasn't too old to cry. She was curled up in a ball on the sofa, next to the electric heater.

'Did he hit you with the chair?' I asked, putting my hand on her shoulder.

'No, no,' she cried, 'It's OK.'

I crossed the room and stood the dining chair up on its feet. I didn't know what to do, or what to say. And I didn't understand what had happened between Mum and Davey. I wondered if Kelly was his wife, and whether Davey was coming back.

Right then I heard a knock at the door. I went through to the kitchen and found Siriol already inside.

'Hello! Sorry it's late, but I wanted to tell you about Tincian......'

She broke off and looked at me with concern, tipping her mop of curly hair on one side, 'You all right Engli...Joel?'

I shook my head slowly, hoping my face didn't show that I felt like crying.

'I saw your Ma's boyfriend. He nearly ran me over, **plon**ker.'

Before I could stop her, Siriol had walked through to the sitting room. In an instant she saw Mum curled up, and knelt on the rug beside her.

'Now what's the **troub**le?' she asked, and her funny emphasis made me feel warm and soothed somehow. I was getting to like her soft way of speaking.

Mum raised her head, and although she hadn't met Siriol before, she didn't seem in the least surprised by her being there.

Siriol went on, 'Now there's nothing so bad as a nice cup of cocoa won't cure,' sounding four times her age, and returning to me in the kitchen.

'Righto Joel, you get the kettle on, and I'll warm the

milk.'

In moments she had stoked the Aga with coal, heated milk in a pan, washed the mugs and set a tray.

We carried the cocoa and biscuits through to Mum.

'D'you know what I think Joel,' she announced, passing the box of tissues to Mum, 'I think this room's a bit de*press*ing. What we need here is a bit of atmosphere.' (She pronounces here and sphere as if they had two parts, hee-yur, and sfee-yur).

She switched off the central light leaving only the lamp, and the room immediately looked more homely.

'Mind if I light a fire in hee-yur?'

Mum sat up and rubbed her wet cheeks, 'No. Does your Dad allow you to light fires?'

Siriol laughed at that, carried logs from the kitchen, cleared the grate and made a start. 'Are you helping?' she asked me, and I knelt down on the hearth-rug as she showed me how to make a small bonfire in the grate of scrunched up newspaper, then lay kindling sticks and place small logs on top. When the paper was lit, she blew gently in the centre and opened the handle at the bottom of the grate. Within a couple of minutes, flames were licking up the chimney.

'A fire makes a home!' she said, pulling up the footstool beside Mum, 'Can you tell me about it?'

I sat at the table and wondered to myself, what is it that women have? And are they born with it, like Siriol? How come she seemed to know what to say and do when they've only just met? I watched and listened in fascination. At least Mum had stopped crying.

'He's gone,' Mum said bleakly.

'Where?'

'Back to Staines. To his wife.'

'Ah - **trick**y. Do you love him?'

'Yes, yes, very much.'

'Well if he loves you, he'll come back. If he doesn't, forget him.'

'We came here together to make a new life, there's nothing for me in Wales without him.' As soon as Mum said that she looked guilty, perhaps realising she was insulting the place where Siriol had grown up.

But if she was offended, Siriol didn't show it, 'That's the way it seems just now because you're upset, but we've got the mountains, and the lake, and all. This is God's own country.' She paused and put a couple of bigger logs on the fire, which was already throwing out a good heat. No-one spoke for a while.

Siriol broke the silence, 'I came to tell Joel about the school bus. For tomorrow.'

Mum looked surprised and rubbed her head distractedly, 'School had gone right out of my mind.' A shadow passed across her face as she added, 'So I'll be on my own all day tomorrow. What if he never comes back? I couldn't bear it!'

I felt a kind of knotty pain in my chest. How come I'm not good enough for Mum? How come the thought of living with me is suddenly so awful? She always used to be OK when it was just the two of us. But I wasn't going to say any of that. Obviously.

Siriol stood up, 'The bus comes through at twenty past eight. Joel, if you call for me at quarter past, we'll walk to the main road together. All the kids on the bus come from local farms and villages, and they're OK. They speak Welsh mostly, but I'll translate.'

I walked with her to the back door.

'Night,' she said, tipping her head on the side, then added

as an afterthought, 'Your Mum doesn't mean to hurt you, she's just upset. It'll be all right in the end.'

'Thanks,' I said, as she disappeared into the cold dark night.

As I lay in bed worrying, I wondered what on earth we're going to live on now Mum doesn't have a job. At least we don't have to pay rent. When we were in Staines I had Gran-Wen and Gramps to share the worry with - but this is the toughest part of not having a Dad. You kind of feel you're responsible for your Mum. But in the back of my mind was the joy of knowing Davey-baby had gone for good.

At breakfast it was obvious Mum was making a superhuman effort to be supportive on my first day at Welsh school.

She looked ashen-white and dead tired, but tried to sound up-beat, 'Everything will be OK at school love, I spoke to your teacher on the phone before we moved, and she sounds lovely. And she'll be very understanding because you don't speak Welsh. You'll be able to take extra language lessons, and Siriol will be a great help.'

'Mmm,' I said, not wanting her to think I agreed with anything she'd just said.

'And I'll be here when you get in from school. What would you like for supper?'

'Anything. Whatever.'

'I feel as though you're blaming me Joel, for coming here, and for.... everything.'

'Well it wasn't my decision. Which pretty much leaves you.'

'I agreed to come because Davey wanted to make a completely fresh start. Away from Staines, and from his...... past.'

'And his wife.'

'That's not fair.'

'It's true. How can you be so thick when it comes to boyfriends? Anyone can see Davey is a jerk. Siriol can. And Gramps.'

Mum looked angry, but sat down and pleaded, 'Let's not argue on your first day at school. If it's any consolation, I'm suffering now for my bad choices. All of them.'

I think she may have been referring to my lack of a Dad, but I didn't want to go there just then.

'It's nearly quarter past eight love, clean your teeth and run down to Siriol's.'

When I gave Mum a kiss on the cheek I still felt angry and hateful towards her. For putting me through this, and for choosing Davey. Because even if my biological Dad was a monster from hell, he couldn't be any worse than Davey.

But as I glanced back over my shoulder at Mum watching me from the cottage doorway, she looked so small and thin that I couldn't help but feel sorry for her. She's had a bum life really. All my friends' mothers have dinner parties and go to yoga and have beauty things done to them in Staines. But Mum's never had any of that, and I reckon they're the things women want. So I made a resolution that I would start giving Mum a better life. Siriol would be able to help me find a paper round or a job as a shepherd's assistant. Or something.

She came out of the farm as soon as I rounded the bend and we jogged to the main road.

'How you feeling?' she asked.

'OK. Bit nervous.'

'My Da's got a great idea. He needs a cleaner in the house, especially now my Mam spends so much time looking after Uncle Gwennol. So he's going to ask your Mam to work for him. He'll pay her.'

'Wow. Thanks.'

An old blue coach flew round the corner and indicated left to stop for us.

'This is **Mor**gan's bus. He drives like a maniac, and he's a chain smoker, but he lets us do whatever we want.'

I stepped up after Siriol, praying she wouldn't embarrass me. It was one of the worst moments of my life. I felt frightened and inadequate. I'm only a year 9 and I could see the back of the bus was full of massive year 10's and 11's.

'Sixty pence. You're new then?' The driver spoke in the very same soft accent as Siriol. He was puffing on a cigarette, which he didn't take out of his mouth when he spoke.

I fished round in my bag, wishing I had known about the 60p and had it ready in advance.

'You can get a bus pass,' he said as he took my money, 'Ask at school.' And he drove away with the coach door still open. I lurched down the aisle and looked for a seat.

'Hee-yur!' Siriol called, pointing to a seat behind her. A small boy with glasses had the window seat, he looked like Harry Potter. I sat next to him.

'Joel this is Emrys,' Siriol said. 'He's year 9 too. Who's your teacher Emrys?'

'Mrs Jones.'

'Same as Joel. You look after him Emrys, all day, and all through dinner, and bring him back to the bus. And help him with the language. If you don't, I'll pull your fingernails out one by one. And it won't be **pre**tty. OK?'

'OK Siriol,' Emrys looked more terrified of Siriol than I was of school. We didn't speak during the journey, while the driver hurtled the coach around every bend, and threw us forward every time he braked. The smell of his cigarette was awful, but maybe in Wales they don't realise smoking gives you cancer.

I could tell Emrys was an OK kid. Not rough, and not a wimp, just OK.

'This is where we get off,' he said, 'Follow me, and I'll take you to Mrs Jones.'

A sign outside the coach window said YSGOL UWCHRADD TYWYN.

'Tywyn Secondary School,' Emrys translated, without me having to ask. 'Well it actually says, School-Secondary-Tywyn.'

We had stopped outside a squat red-brick building, fronted by a lawn, and bordered by grey buildings that seemed to belong to the school. Kids were arriving in twos and threes, and to be honest, they looked all right. Not as fashionable as the kids at my school in Staines, and I was glad about that. I couldn't spot many designer bags, and some of the haircuts would have been called well-sad in London.

On and off during the day I saw Siriol, once in a corridor, a couple of times at break. And Emrys stuck to me like glue. He was small, quiet and kind, and obviously terrified Siriol would break his kneecaps if he didn't look after me.

Although loads of the kids spoke Welsh all the time, some spoke English. And the lessons were a mixture of both languages. Mrs Jones is young and strict, but fair. She introduced me to the class in the usual way, 'This is Joel and I want you to be very friendly, and help him find his way around the school. He's new to Welsh, and we'll all be using English to make him feel at home. Won't we Ewan Jones? And don't even think about flicking your rubber at Emrys, or you'll be straight to Mr *Ev*ans.'

At break I thought about what Mrs Jones had said, and

her words made me remember something terrible. In the final half term of year 7, a new boy had started at Ryton High. On his first day, our teacher had read us the riot act about being nice to him, and Stuart and I were assigned as 'foster-friends' to help him settle in.

Until now I had blocked all memories of this phase of my life. Now the shameful recollections flooded back into my brain - as I stood in the dinner queue it all came rushing back. How Stuart and I had deliberately played hide and seek with the new boy, so he could never find us, and so he got lost all over school. How we pretended his Mum had telephoned and we sent him on a wild goose-chase to the staff room, and lied about the way to the science block so he was ten minutes late for his first science lesson.

We nicked his packed lunch and Gary ate it in front of him, while the new boy went hungry. I suddenly remembered how I had pushed my nose under his, and murmured, 'Mmm, yum, you must be soooo hungry'.

He left after a week and a half. And no-one ever punished me or Stuart. For the last year or two I had buried these memories and tried to forget I had done these things. And now, as I chose my lunch of Welsh sausages and chips, I realised *I* was the new boy. And all these Welsh kids were being really kind.

They didn't care if I had an iPod or a camera-phone. As soon as I approached a group of boys, they stopped speaking Welsh and began to speak English, so I could understand. I felt completely ashamed of how I had behaved at Ryton High.

'You all right?' Emrys suddenly asked me.

His eyes looked worried behind the round Harry Potter glasses.

'Yup, I'm fine. And... thanks,' I added, truly meaning it.

How was it?' Mum asked me, as we walked up our track towards the cottage. 'I've been looking out for the coach since half past three.'

'Fine.'

Then Siriol butted in, dancing round me and walking backwards in front of my Mum, 'He had a good day. Emrys looked after him, and everyone says Joel's cool.'

'That's nice.'

'Fancy a cup of tea?' she asked us, pointing towards the farm.

'No thanks, but another time,' Mum replied, and Siriol waved as she turned into the farmyard.

Our cottage looked brighter inside somehow. It may have been the sun shining through the little windows, or it may have been cleaned. I could smell fresh paint coming from somewhere.

Mum said, 'I painted your room, it looks so much better. And there's some wonderful news - Siriol's Dad asked me to work for him as a cleaner.'

'Yeah, Siriol said.'

'I'll start by doing four hours a week... it's funny, we should be paying Mr Jones rent, but he's going to be paying me instead!'

I could tell Mum was trying really hard to be cheerful, and she hadn't even mentioned Davey-baby. I put down my school bag and threw my arms round her neck.

'That's better,' she said, squeezing me.

'Joel! Joel!' came a shriek from the lane.

Siriol crashed through the kitchen door and grabbed my

arm, 'Uncle Gwennol's found Tincian!'

'Chinks!' I blurted.

'Pardon?' asked Mum.

I felt my heart leap inside my chest, it must have jumped a full five centimetres.

'Let's go!' Siriol urged me, tugging my sleeve.

'Wait! Where are you going, and how long for?' Mum asked.

'Abergynolwyn, an hour, on the bikes,' Siriol called over her shoulder as we ran.

'Be careful, for goodness sake. Tea at five-thirty Jo-Jo,' Mum called after us.

It was difficult to talk as we pedalled along the road towards the village, I've realised I'm not as fit as Siriol. Yet.

But she did yell, 'Don't forget to say you lost Tincian.'

I wasn't sure how I was going to carry this off, and hoped Siriol would do the talking.

Uncle Gwennol's front door was open, and he came out slowly to greet us, leaning on his walking stick and wearing a waxed jacket, 'Don't bother taking off your boots, Tincian's up the valley - we'll go by car.'

I rode in the back of Gwennol's veterinary van which was filthy and messy. He didn't wear a seat belt, and drove a bit like Morgan on the coach.

He said, 'The phone call came at lunchtime, from an old couple I've known for years. They farm close to the coast.'

I was longing for Gwennol to tell me more details. And worried in case the dog didn't turn out to be the real Chinks.

Siriol sang song lyrics as we bounced along the lanes, she hadn't a care in the world, as if she knew everything would turn out right. And for her, it always seems to. I watched her curls of red hair bouncing on the back of her neck, and two small hands drumming on the dashboard as she sang out, 'Woah, woah, she's the one!'

Gwennol joined in with his deep bass voice.

I had a weird feeling inside, and wasn't sure what it was. I glanced from Siriol to the back of her uncle's head, and suddenly it came to me. Family. This felt like family. This is what it must feel like to be in the back of a car with your Dad.

The van swerved into a lane, bumped along and came to an abrupt halt.

Gwennol swung himself down and called a greeting towards the building. It was yet another grey stone cottage, with small snug windows tucked just beneath a grey slate roof.

Immediately I heard the high-pitched bark of a dog, followed by a second much deeper bark.

An elderly woman came out of the cottage, wiping her hands on a piece of cloth that was tied round her middle like an apron. Her grey hair was tied in a loose bun, and she spoke Welsh to Gwennol. He replied, using the same soft musical tones, so it sounded almost as if they were singing lines of a song, first one of them, then the other.

Meanwhile, Siriol darted about, like a little bird hopping from branch to branch.

'What are they saying?' I asked her.

She seemed totally relaxed, while my heart was beating in my chest like a drum. Worries were going round and round in my head, in case this turned out to be the wrong dog, and I had to offend Gwennol and the old Welsh woman.

'She says she found the dog by the road..... My uncle asked was he wearing a collar.'

As we talked, the woman led us behind the farmhouse

towards a grey stone barn. Then the high-pitched barking began again.

'She says Chinks is in the pig-pen,' Siriol explained.

I was thinking - in a few seconds I'll see the dog. In a few seconds it will all be final. And that scared me.

The woman turned to me and said in a thick accent, 'You must be glad to find him. He's a lovely dog, a very friendly one.'

She opened the barn door and led us into the dark interior, it smelled of straw and animals. The barking intensified, and I remember seeing a sow in the first stall with lots of piglets snuffling her under-belly, then an empty stall, then everything else faded away, because Chinks was looking up at me, his white front paws supporting him as he tried to see over the wall of the pen.

'Chinks!' I yelled, and he immediately jumped towards me, almost managing to vault out of the pen in his excitement.

The woman opened the gate to let me in, and at last I was cuddling him, as he wriggled in my arms and licked my hands, face and ears. I was taking in the softness of his ears and the thump of his stumpy tail as if it would wag right off.

'Hurray!' Siriol was cheering, 'I knew you'd find him,' and at that moment I realised we hadn't actually told any fibs, because I've been searching for Chinks all my life.

You'll be needing a new collar and lead,' Gwennol said over his shoulder as the van bumped its way back towards Abergynolwyn.

'I've got the collar at home,' I said, lifting my nose from Chinks' smooth head for a moment. He was riding on my knee, and watching the view outside intently, ears forward, wet nose sniffing. We saw a sheepdog and immediately he growled.

Gwennol laughed, 'That's a true Jack Russell..... you won't be able to walk him off the lead here, if he sees another dog he'll just run for it, never mind if there's a lorry coming.'

I ran my finger down the white stripe between his eyes, and tickled him underneath both tan coloured ears. The softness of his fur was impossible to describe.

Now and again Siriol looked at me and grinned, she was just so happy about me finding Chinks.

'You need to rest now,' she said to Gwennol as he parked the van. 'Mam will be along later with your supper.'

'I'll just find a lead for Joel, and give the dog a quick check-up. Follow me,' he said and went into his house.

I carried Chinks in my arms.

'Through here!' Gwennol called from a small room on the left of the hall.

'That's the consulting room,' Siriol explained.

'Pop him up on the table,' said Gwennol, washing his hands in a big sink on the wall. He turned the long tap handle on and off with his elbow.

Chinks was good as gold while Gwennol examined him. My eyes were taking in every tiny detail of him, his brown ears, white stripe down the middle of his face, brownish-black tail, and dark shiny eyes. The fur around his right eye was white, and around the left was brown, and I noticed that his eyelashes matched, one set were white, the other brown. The whole of his body was white, and his pink tummy was marked with big freckles which showed through the thin fur on his under-belly.

Gwennol took his temperature (that looked painful), peered in his mouth and ears, listened to his chest with a stethoscope, and felt his tummy, and all over the body.

'He's about two years old isn't he?' Gwennol asked as he examined Chinks' teeth.

'Um,' I hesitated.

'Well, he's sound as a whistle anyway. Is he up to date with his vaccinations?'

'He hasn't had any,' I stammered, the question catching me completely by surprise.

'I'll give him a booster, just in case.'

I was worried when I saw the needle, but Gwennol was so quick, that I don't think Chinks realised he'd had an injection. Gwennol rubbed the scruff of his neck where the needle had been, and Chinks asked to get down.

'That's saved you a few quid,' Siriol said.

'I'll pay you back,' I said to her uncle, 'I'm going to get a job as soon as I can.'

'Not necessary, it's my gift. Bring the collar back next time,' he said, fixing it around Chinks' neck and attaching the lead. 'He'll probably be very happy running beside your bike, but pull in at the roadside whenever a car tries to pass. We don't want any accidents now you've found each other again.'

'I don't know how to...... thank you..... properly,' I

106

stammered.

'No need to, your smiling face is thanks enough,' Gwennol said, patting me on the shoulder as we left.

'Put the lead over the handlebar,' Siriol suggested, 'and you go first, I'll follow.'

Thankfully there weren't many cars on the road. Siriol pedalled slowly and at first Chinks tried to jump up to me, but he soon got the right idea, and galloped beside my wheels. With his ears pressed back, and tail up, he seemed to be loving the run. Whenever Siriol heard a vehicle approaching, she pulled in, and I tugged the lead to bring Chinks against the verge. We got home without a mishap.

'What will your Mam say?' Siriol asked.

'Dunno. She said I wasn't allowed a dog, Davey hates them.'

'He's not here.'

'True.'

'See you tomorrow then, quarter past eight for the bus,' she smiled. 'And Joel, I'm so happy for you.'

I leaned the bike against the wall, led Chinks on his lead and pushed the kitchen door open gingerly. Mum was cooking on the Aga.

'Um, Mum?' I began.

'Yes love.'

But Chinks was too keen, and pushed past me on the lead, straining on his collar to reach Mum. His tail was wagging madly.

'Joel, what the heck - is this Siriol's dog?'

'This is Chinks.'

'What on earth have you done? You didn't ask me,' she protested, but couldn't help squatting down and patting him. He licked her hands and wagged frantically.

'You're a friendly one,' she said, then stood and changed her tone to cross. 'Joel, where did you get this dog?'

'From Siriol's Uncle Gwennol.'

This was definitely a case of giving short answers, I find that if I say less, eventually the adult gets bored of trying.

'Is it his dog?'

'No.'

'Well whose then?'

'Someone found him.'

'Look, you can't waltz in here with a strange dog, and expect me to accept it. I never said you could have a dog, he'll have to go back.'

'No!' I wailed.

'How can we afford to feed him, and buy a bed, and.... everything? And what on earth am I supposed to do with him while you're at school every day. It won't do Joel, it won't do.'

As soon as Mum raised her voice, Chinks' tail went down, his ears back, and he moved close to my legs.

'He's scared,' I pleaded, 'don't be cross with us.'

'Oh for heaven's sake,' Mum said, turning her back to me and slamming the pan about.

I stood rooted to the spot, calculating whether I could get to the sitting room without causing another outburst.

Suddenly Mum turned to face me, waving her wooden spoon. Little drops of sauce flicked into the air as she spoke. 'Do you have his number?'

'Who?'

'Uncle Gwennol.'

'No.'

'Well, I'm going to get it,' she said decisively, putting down her spoon and strutting out of the back door. I wasn't completely sure how she was feeling. She seemed cross, but not mad, a bit angry, but not the raging, screaming kind. I reckoned she would come round in time.

Thinking it might be pushing my luck to take Chinks up to my newly painted bedroom, I undid his lead, and let him into the sitting room. I wanted to play with him, but he was too busy sniffing. He sniffed right round the edges of the room, the rug, even in the cold fireplace. It seemed to be his method of finding out, in the way that I might read a piece of paper to find out facts, he was reading with his nose. His sniffing was very quick and shallow, and his nose was always about two millimetres from the surface. There was one place on the skirting board that seemed to be driving him mad, and he blew out snorts and snuffs of air at that place. I wondered if there might be a mouse on the other side.

'Here, come here boy!' I encouraged, but he wasn't going to respond.

Suddenly his attention was diverted. He came towards the sofa and put his paws on it.

'Down!' I said, knowing Mum wouldn't like him on the furniture.

He was staring at Mum's teddy, the disgusting one Davey-baby had given her, with a big red heart sewn on its belly and the words 'SQUEEZE ME'.

He wasn't going to take his eyes off the teddy, and he began to make small whining noises in the back of his throat.

'No, leave it!' I said.

Perhaps I could distract him with food, and I ventured into the kitchen to find a biscuit. I was only gone a moment, and when I came back with the biscuit tin, Chinks was nowhere to be seen.

'Chinks!' I called and looked behind the sofa. There he

was, ears down, Mum's soppy teddy in his mouth.

Mum chose that exact moment to return.

'Drop it!' I hissed. 'Drop it!' and Chinks whizzed past me into the kitchen with his prize.

'He's got my teddy!' she yelped.

'Sorry Mum, I'll get it,' I said.

I grabbed his collar and tried to pull the teddy out of his mouth, but Chinks' jaw was so strong that I knew the material would tear before he let go. So I produced a biscuit.

He looked confused, lowered the teddy for a moment, then changed his mind and stared at the biscuit, teddy between his teeth.

As I moved the food nearer to his face, hunger must have got the better of him, because he opened his mouth and I retrieved the teddy. It had slimey spit all over it.

'Sorry,' I said again.

Mum was dialling from her mobile.

'Hello, yes I'm Joel's mother, and I'm ringing about the dog.... Yes that's right.... So he says.'

That was the moment I realised my story about losing Chinks was about to be exposed. And there was nothing at all I could do about it. So I bent down and picked up Chinks, letting my nose breathe in the gorgeous smell of his soft ears, the scent of cosiness, and spice, and heaven.

'He didn't have a dog, no,' Mum was saying on the phone, 'he's never had one..... mmm.... I see, well it will have to go back.' There was a pause, then, 'Until the owner turns up, yes, I suppose so. That's very good of you, yes..... And I've heard all about you from the children. Yes, thanks, Bye then.'

I didn't look up, but lowered my face deeper into Chinks' white fur. Waited for the explosion.

But Mum's reaction shocked me. Instead of yelling, she

crouched on the floor beside me and began to stroke Chinks thoughtfully.

'Joel,' she began, 'we need to talk. I know how much you've longed for a dog - ever since you were a toddler. Do you remember the toy one you made out of my old tights? It was lumpy and not very dog-like, but you dragged it round the flat on a piece of string for weeks. And you made it a bed from a Weetabix box.' She smiled and went on stroking Chinks.

'And I also know how tough the move from Staines is for you, missing your friends, and Gran-Wen, and Gramps. But you've told a dreadful lie to Uncle Gwennol. If you hadn't done that, I may have let you keep Chinks, but now it won't be possible.'

A tear wanted to escape from my squeezed up eyes, and I held Chinks even closer. Why had I let Gwennol think I had lost a dog? But if Mum had allowed me to have a dog in the first place, there would have been no lie - it was all so completely unfair.

'If you'd let me have a dog when I asked, this wouldn't have happened,' I pleaded, 'and I never told an actual lie, Uncle Gwennol assumed I'd lost my dog, and we just... let him think it.'

'I've always taught you to be truthful, that's what hurts me most in all this. But we need to find a way forward. I've told Uncle Gwennol that you can look after Chinks until the real owner is found. And if you're very good, then we can consider you having a dog of your own after that.'

'I don't want another dog. I want Chinks,' I said.

'This isn't your dog love. That's why it would have been much better to go about things in the right way, by involving me, and not telling lies.'

'What if no-one comes for him?' I asked hopefully.

'They will Joel, that's inevitable.'

'I'll pray,' I said. 'And it'll work, 'because I prayed for help when we arrived here and Chinks turned up a few days later.'

'But we don't believe in God Joel, you're not even christened.'

'Well I'm going to pray anyway,' I said.

At least I was able to stop Mum worrying about the cost of a dog-bed - we put Chinks to sleep on my old fleece on the rug in front of the Aga. That was after he had eaten our leftover supper.

'I'll buy some dog food in Tywyn tomorrow,' Mum promised.

And Chinks had distracted Mum from thinking about Davey-baby too much. I noticed instead of staring into space while we watched TV, or checking her mobile every other minute, she kept looking at the dog instead. I had spent the entire evening playing ball, chasing him round the sitting room, and stroking him. I couldn't even tell you what programmes were on that evening.

Everything had gone well until bedtime. Chinks had even asked to go outside for a wee by whining at the back door, and hadn't got on Mum's nerves at all.

'Night-night,' I said, stroking him and tucking the fleece around his legs, knowing the Aga would stay warm all night. 'Will you be OK with the light off?'

As I climbed the stairs to bed, Chinks was silent. Just as I reached the top stair, he let out one small bark. Then he waited.

I went into my room, 'The paint looks nice,' I called to Mum.

'That dog had better not bark all night,' she called back.

Right on cue, he let out two short, sharp yaps.

'I'll go!' I called, but Mum stuck her head out of her room, 'No Joel, you have to leave him, or he'll know that barking works. It's like a baby crying to be picked up. There's nothing wrong with him.'

We stood at the top of the stairs, Mum wrapping her dressing gown around her bare arms. Soon the barking became more frantic, and was interspersed with whines and cries.

'He's in a state, I have to go to him,' I begged.

'No Joel, leave him!'

'What if he's poo'ed on the floor, or been sick?' I asked her, 'Or he's chewing the door?'

Mum paused very briefly and then said, 'All right, go and see.'

Chinks was off his bed, his face squashed up to the sitting room door.

He stuck to my legs like glue as I walked back to the bottom of the stairs.

'He wants to come up,' I called to Mum.

I could see her patience was wearing thin.

Chinks wagged his stumpy tail slowly and tipped his head on one side.

'I give up!' she said, and went into her bedroom.

We bounded up the stairs two at a time and dived onto my bed. Chinks went through the sniffing routine, and then rolled around on my duvet, wagging his tail and licking my ears.

'Now settle down!' I laughed at him, turning off the light. For a moment he was completely still and alert, listening for noises, then he snuggled up to my chest through the duvet, and put his head in the crook of my arm. In a few moments he was asleep.

The second day at school was better than the first in every way. I had my 60p ready for Morgan on the bus in advance, I had Emrys to sit next to, and Chinks to look forward to all day in lessons. I was so excited I could hardly concentrate.

Just as the bus rounded the last bend on our journey home, Siriol leaned over the seat and prodded me, 'Hey, did you see the news last night? On BBC One.'

'I was playing with Chinks.'

'There was something on it you should see. I heard Mam and Da talking about it in the kitchen while they were making supper, so I video'd it for you on the ten o'clock.'

'Was it about dogs?'

'No, *stu*ped - sorry - it was about....' She paused, beckoned me towards her mouth and whispered, 'about finding out who your Da is.'

We stood in the bus aisle, bracing ourselves ready for Morgan to slam the brakes on at the end of our track.

'What did your Mum say?' I asked her. For a moment, the thought of seeing Chinks had been pushed to the back of my mind.

'They had the telly on in the kitchen. Mam said to Da, 'Do you think Joel's Da could be one of those?' and Da said, 'Well it won't affect him will it, the legislation isn't regressive or retrogressive, or something like that.'

I hadn't got a clue what she was on about. We climbed down the steps and waved to Emrys.

'Come round later and watch the video - I expect you want to see Chinks first.'

'Yeah, I do,' I said, just as Mum came into view with Chinks on the lead. He had spotted me and was straining, choking at his throat, so eager to see me. Mum bent down and set him free. He bounded up to us and when he reached me, he jumped right off the ground into my arms.

'Ah!' cooed Siriol, 'Look how he loves you!'

He wriggled and flailed in my arms with excitement until I put him down again.

'You'll have to be careful with him when there are sheep around,' Mum said. 'I had real trouble on our walk, he was all right while they stood still, but as soon as one of them runs he goes crazy.'

'Thanks for walking him,' I said.

'It did me good, and I spent a couple of hours working for your parents Siriol, so I'm fit as a fiddle,' she smiled. Mum looked better than she had for weeks, her eyes were bright and alive, instead of the worried look she's had since Davey-baby came into her life.

'Can Joel come and watch a video?' Siriol asked Mum.

'Of course, have you got any homework?'

'No,' we both replied in unison.

'Sure? Supper at six Jo-Jo.'

'Bring Chinks,' Siriol said to me.

We decided to introduce Chinks to Chicklet on our way. I felt suddenly guilty, remembering that I hadn't bothered with her for a couple of days. She wasn't in her hutch, and I realised I hadn't put her away on Sunday night. Chinks went right inside the hutch and sniffed for England. Especially at the piles of chicken poo.

'What if the fox has got her?' I asked Siriol.

'Don't be daft, she'll be fine.'

We looked for her in the farmyard, where Chinks tried

to chase the hens, which made both the sheepdogs pull on their chains and bark at him. He strained at the lead and tried to look extra fierce, but they were a lot bigger and scarier than him.

'She's not in the yard,' Siriol announced, scrambling into the open barn. A cluster of white doves flew out, circling and dancing in the air above us. Chinks loved climbing in the straw. It tickled his nose and made him sneeze as he lolloped about.

'Here she is!' yelled Siriol, pointing upwards, then putting her finger to her lips, 'Ssshhh, she's sitting on a nest. Hey you might have some chicks soon Joel.'

Chicklet had made herself a cosy nook in the straw and was sitting puffed out and flat.

Very carefully, Siriol felt underneath her body and came back to me. 'There are four eggs!'

Mrs Jones called out 'Hello,' as we went through the kitchen. She didn't bat an eyelid about us bringing Chinks indoors. That's what I like about farm life. Muddy boots and dog hairs are fine. You can enjoy yourself, without worrying about Dettol and germs.

'I didn't understand much of this news story,' Siriol warned me as she pushed the video into the slot, 'But I reckon it may give us a clue about your Da. You could ask your Mam about it.'

She pressed PLAY.

The BBC newsreader began to speak. Behind her was a picture of a tiny baby lying on a sheet.

'Donor fathers are about to lose their anonymity, the government has announced in a statement today. The changes are a result of a two-year public consultation on the amount of information children of donors should have access to.'

I looked at Siriol who was biting her fingernail. She seemed intent.

'Children of donors will be able to have pen portraits of their parent, which would detail their eye and hair colour, occupation and religion. Supporters say children conceived in this way have a right to information about their genetic parents. The changes will come into force from April 2005, however they will not be retrospective for children born before this date.'

The picture behind the newsreader changed and she began to talk about Iraq.

'What did all that mean?' I asked Siriol.

'Dunno, but it may be about you and your Da. You know we talked about clowning the other day?'

'Cloning.'

'Whatever. And you've got no Da right? Well I've been thinking, and there are only a few ways of making a baby.'

She made one hand into a fist and stuck up one finger.

'First, the normal way, by a man and a woman who are married...... you know.'

I nodded quickly, to shut her up. Chinks was looking at her with his head on one side.

She held up a second finger, 'Two, by having a baby in a test tube, that's clowning.'

I didn't correct her this time.

'And three, by immaculate conception.'

'You what?'

'Like Jesus. Mary had Jesus by immaculate conception, she didn't have a husband and God helped her.... have a baby, without a Dad, by a miracle.'

I must have looked blank.

'Come on Joel, you must have heard this in church enough times.'

'I've never been to church.'

Siriol looked horrified, 'Poor you. Well God is Jesus' Father, and Mary is his mother, and so she's the only woman who had a baby without........ S. E. X. or test tubes.'

'Could that have happened to my Mum?'

'No way, God only had one son. And he never had a daughter either.' She was looking at me so seriously, and seemed to care genuinely about my search for a Dad.

There was a knock at the door and Uncle Gwennol stepped into the TV lounge. I hoped he hadn't heard what we'd been saying.

He spoke softly just like Siriol, 'Hello you two, and you mate,' as he rubbed Chinks' head. 'I'm having supper here tonight and thought I'd stick my head in to say hello.'

'Uncle Gwennol?' Siriol said in a very meaningful way.

I had a terrible suspicion that I knew what she was going to say next.

'Can we show you something from the news?'

Oh no! I thought, oh flipping no!

'Of course you can, I'll sit myself down.'

She rewound the video and paused it before the item. Chinks climbed onto my lap and tucked his head down. I kept quiet as a mouse.

'Did you know Joel hasn't got a Da?'

'Well yes, I realised that.'

'Well, his Mam says he just hasn't got one, and never had one, and we know everyone has a Da.'

Gwennol looked a bit uncomfortable.

'We've done it in Biology, even I did it in year 7. And I've just been telling Joel that there's only three ways to have a baby - a man and a woman the normal way,' she looked down and pulled a bit of fluff off her sock, 'or in a test tube, or immaculate conception.'

Gwennol smiled broadly, then rubbed his hand across his mouth, as if he was trying to wipe away the smile.

'Well yes, that's about it,' he said.

'We need you to explain this video to us, because we think it might help Joel find his Da.'

Gwennol turned to me and looked very kindly into my eyes, 'Perhaps the first thing is for you to ask your Mam about this Joel.'

'I have,' I said.

'OK, hasn't that helped?' Gwennol asked.

I shook my head.

The newsreader began again, 'Donor fathers are about to lose their anonymity, the government has announced in a statement today. The changes are a result of a two-year public consultation on the amount of information children of donors should have access to.'

'Hang on, press pause,' Gwennol said. He looked very thoughtful. 'I'm a medical man, and I've been trained for this kind of.... situation, so let me try and explain for you.

'If I give you a bit of background, then we'll be able to make more sense of the news story. You're right about the three ways of having a child, but they're a bit more complicated than you thought.' He stared at the wall and rubbed his chin thoughtfully, 'First a man and a woman can conceive a child by making love, having sex, where the child is created naturally from the egg and the sperm.'

We had heard about this, no problem here. It would be OK as long as he didn't ask us any questions, or make us talk about it. In class, the boys hate having to answer questions with the words about boys' bits, and the girls won't answer the questions with words about girls' bits. It's just too embarrassing.

Gwennol went on, 'But the second way is the complicated one. Sometimes, if a man and woman are having trouble getting pregnant by themselves, the doctors can help them out. They do this by taking the egg and the sperm out of the parents bodies, fertilising them in a test tube, then when the baby is first formed, they pop it back into the mother's womb, and it grows there just like any other baby.'

'So that's clowning?' Siriol asked.

'She means cloning,' I explained.

Gwennol coughed away a laugh and rubbed his mouth again. His eyes were still smiling.

'No, cloning is different. Cloning is a very new idea, where doctors and scientists are trying to split a newly formed baby and make it into two exact copies, a bit like twins. They don't do it with humans yet, only with animals, like sheep.'

'That's what I said!' Siriol burst out, 'Someone is making a new sheep out of bits of a dead sheep.'

'They're a long way from that yet, but one day doctors may be able to re-create a life from body tissues. It's not something I agree with, because it goes against the laws of creation in my view. Now back to the news item. Usually test-tube babies are made for a man and a woman who can't have a baby by themselves. But also a woman can have a test-tube baby even if she hasn't got a partner.'

'Why would anyone do that?' I asked.

'Lots of reasons, they might not have a husband.... Um...' Gwennol looked stumped.

I blurted out, 'But that's so selfish - to try and have a baby when there isn't a Dad! It isn't fair on the baby!'

Gwennol and Siriol were silent.

Then the penny dropped, 'My Mum would never have done that. She just wouldn't.'

Gwennol looked really bothered, 'Joel, you must talk this through with your Mum. There are other ways of having a child too, and by far the most common of those is to adopt. Couples can adopt, and so can a single parent, so you see, it's all fairly complicated.'

'Can you explain the news story now?' Siriol urged.

Her uncle looked tired, 'Yes, but I'm not implying that this is how you were made Joel, or anything of the kind. I'll just explain the news item. The news-reader announced that after taking advice from lots of people, the government has decided children who were conceived in a test-tube will have the right to know some basic details about their biological parents.'

Siriol pressed PLAY.

The news continued, 'Children of donors will be able to have pen portraits of their parent, which would detail their eye and hair colour, occupation and religion. Supporters say children conceived in this way have a right to information about their genetic parents. The changes will come into force from April 2005, however they will not be retrospective for children born before this date.'

We looked at Gwennol again.

He said, 'That's saying the new law won't apply to any baby born before April 2005.'

'So it won't help me then,' I said blankly, 'I was born in 1991.'

'Talk to your Mam Joel, that's my advice,' Gwennol said kindly, 'and remember what I said – there are lots of different ways of having a baby.'

'And no ways of getting a Dad,' I said under my breath.

I had absolutely no intention of speaking to Mum about this. Because she's blown every chance she's ever had to tell me about my elusive Dad.

All that evening as I played ball with Chinks, and all that night as I woke and snuggled closer to his soft fur, I wondered whether Mum could have stooped low enough to having a baby when she didn't have a Dad for it.

I had so many questions.

Did my Mum and Dad know each other?

Am I adopted?

Was I made in a test tube?

Why would any Mum want a baby that way – without a real Dad?

And why in the name of David Beckham would any man want to create a baby he was never going to see?

None of this made any sense at all, but I began to wonder about the bloke who is walking round the world, probably somewhere in England, who is biologically my Dad.

And has he ever thought about who he has created?

What does he look like? Does he have straight brown hair like me? Blue eyes? Was he any good at rugby? Could it be Jonny Wilkinson?

That night I think I hated Mum for a few hours, and was far angrier with her than I'd ever been about Davey, or about moving to Wales. And I didn't know what I was going to do with all the feelings that were building up in my chest.

At three am, just when I thought I was going to burst with pain, Chinks woke up, and licked me on the nose, as if he was trying to say, 'Hey, don't worry, I'm here.'

As I squeezed him, a new fear rose inside me, the fear that Chinks' owner might come looking for him. There was only one thing for it, 'Er God,' I said aloud, 'Excuse me for asking, but please could you make sure I keep Chinks for ever. Amen.'

School was getting better every day. A group of lads in my year play football at lunch break on the sports field, and they had let me join in. Emrys watched us from the sidelines, once or twice he agreed to be goalie, but he wasn't much good. He was turning out to be a reliable mate though, and whenever I passed Siriol in a corridor or the dinner queue, she beamed and winked.

Once as we passed each other I heard one of her friends asking, 'Who's your good-looking friend?' That made me feel great.

'Can we take Chinks for a walk?' I asked Siriol as we stepped off Morgan's bus that afternoon. I didn't want to spend a whole evening with Mum. I hadn't forgiven her yet for what she might have done to have a baby, and I wanted time to think.

'Yeah, let's take him to the quarry,' Siriol suggested.

'Where's that?'

'Nant Gwernol, behind Abergynolwyn.'

We pedalled on the bikes, letting Chinks run beside me on the lead - he was now an expert.

Once we reached the village, Siriol said we would abandon the bikes, 'It's really steep after this,' she said.

'If we had mountain bikes, we wouldn't have to walk,' I said grumpily.

'So you stay here and look at a postcard of the quarry instead of walking, you big girl!'

I wasn't going to be laughed at by a year 8 redhead, and shouted, 'Race you to the top!'

That was a big mistake. As soon as we began to follow the path out of the village beside the narrow-gauge railway line, I knew I'd taken on more than I could handle. Chinks was bounding ahead of us up the footpath, and Siriol was catching me every second.

Just as she passed me I stopped, grabbed my leg and yelled, 'Aaaaaargh!'

She ran on for a few metres then stopped and called back, 'You don't fool me.'

'My leg! My leg!' I said, pulling a pained face. Pathetic really, I don't know why I couldn't let her think she'd beaten me.

'You all right?' she asked, uncertain now.

'I think so.'

After a short walk along a tree-lined gully, we reached a tiny railway station, perched on a narrow ledge high above the ravine. Everything was shut up and it felt weird, as though lots of people were very near, almost close enough to see and hear, but not quite. They wouldn't be wearing modern clothes, but old-fashioned breeches and hats. I could picture them so clearly, even though I don't know anything about history.

'Siriol!'

'*Ie*,' she said absent-mindedly, using the Welsh for 'yes'. I was getting used to it, and hardly noticed her occasional Welsh words.

'This might sound weird, but I can sort of imagine people here, but in old-fashioned clothes.'

'That's not weird,' she replied, sitting down on the platform edge and swinging her legs as she spoke, 'I feel that too.'

A bird was singing near us, pouring out a song so sweet and musical that I could feel it in my chest, the sound was beautiful, but achingly sad.

'This place makes me feel….. *trist,* in a nice way, inside,' she said, putting her fist on her heart. 'Right here is where the little wagons, full of slate from the quarry above us, were lowered down by ropes to join the railway bound for the coast. The rails are still up there, plunging down into the ravine, they're useless now. They began quarrying about a hundred and fifty years ago, and it was a hard, dangerous life for the miners. After they'd mined most of the slate, the inside got more and more unstable, and eventually, on Boxing Day in 1846, the whole mine collapsed.'

'Can we go up there and see?'

'Yes, but it's not a walk for wimps with bad legs.'

I tried to shove her, but she was too quick, jumping to her feet and running along the platform.

She hadn't lied about the walk, it was more of a rock-climb than a ramble. Chinks loved it, but the backs of my legs were burning by the time we reached the quarry. The landscape opened up in front of us to reveal gashes where the mines had been long ago. It was the sort of dangerous place Mum would hate me to be, and I felt she deserved that, today of all days.

We had disturbed a massive black bird from its perch. It flapped away from us, flying only twenty centimetres from the ground, the tips of its shiny black wings almost stroking the surface as it powered away. Then it rose and soared above us.

'A Raven,' Siriol identified.

'It's massive! Huge!' I said.

'Like an eagle,' she added.

Chinks bounded over rocks and boulders, until he reached a high ledge. Suddenly I remembered the film I had seen years ago, about the dog trapped in the Mexican mineshaft.

'Chinks!' I yelled, 'Come back!'

'He'll be OK,' Siriol said, 'they have a sixth sense about danger.'

We watched him picking his way along the ledge, leaning over, sniffing, moving dangerously near to the edge. Then, to my horror, a rock gave way under his feet, starting a little landslide of stones clattering down to us beneath him.

'No!' I screamed, but Chinks had more sense than I thought, and jumped away from the edge just in time. Suddenly I wanted to be away from the place, with Chinks safe beside me.

He bounded back to us, 'Let's go home,' I said.

Mum was in the kitchen of our cottage, and I knew I was really late for supper. I braced myself for the rocketing, wiped Chinks' feet on the old towel and hung my coat on the peg. I noticed a small tear on the elbow. Oh no, my school coat, that spelled disaster. I tucked the sleeve out of sight and hoped she wouldn't notice.

'I had a phone call while you were at school,' Mum said, 'Come and sit down.'

She carried her cup of tea into the sitting room. Chinks was shattered from the walk and collapsed in front of the fire immediately.

'It was Uncle Gwennol. He told me about your little chat last night at the farm.'

My heart missed a beat. Why are adults so completely

impossible to trust? Why do they let you down? Even the nice ones like Gwennol.

'He said a lot of things, but the main reason for ringing was to give me a bit of a lecture. Which I probably deserve.' She paused and took a sip of tea, playing with her mug nervously.

I have to admit, she looked nearly as uncomfortable as I felt.

'You've often asked me about your Dad, and I've always refused to talk about it. And to be honest Joel, I still feel the same. But Gwennol has made me realise that this isn't just about me, it's about you too.'

Well abby-dabby-dooflip! I thought, it's only taken you fourteen years to work that out.

'And I've been wrong in thinking I could keep the details private. But, they're very painful to me, and I've always felt you were too young to know. Is it OK if we just leave it for now?'

'I s'pose,' I said, feeling I had no choice.

'And I promise to talk to you before too long.'

'Why can't you talk to me now? It's not fair that you decide everything... when it's about *my* Dad.'

Just at that moment, Mum's mobile rang, and I could tell from the way she leapt to her feet, that she hoped it was Davey.

'Oh, it's Gwennol,' she said disappointedly as she saw the caller ID, 'Hello! Yes, it's Caitlin.......'

Then her face changed again, and I saw a shadow pass across her eyes.

'Oh dear, yes of course, I'll tell him.'

'Tell me what?' I asked anxiously.

'Joel, this is bad news. Gwennol says Chinks' owner has

come forward, and he wants the dog back.'

iriol couldn't tell me anything new. I didn't even care that she saw me in tears, nothing mattered any more. Suddenly it didn't matter if my Dad was an axe murderer, or if I never find out where I come from for the rest of my life. Because I'd found the one thing in my life I had ever wanted, and was about to lose him.

'We'll make this right Joel,' Siriol said as we sat in her TV lounge. She was missing *Eastenders* to listen to me. That's true friendship.

'Do you want me to phone Uncle Gwennol for you?'

I nodded half-heartedly, and she fetched the phone. As soon as she got through, she passed the handset to me.

'Hullo' I said, not really wanting to speak, but knowing I had to find out the worst.

'Hello Joel, I realise this is terrible news for you, and I'm hoping we can find a way through. It's a pity you and Siriol led me to believe Chinks was your dog from the start, but that doesn't help us now.'

'He *IS* my dog,' I insisted, 'we just hadn't found each other yet.'

'Yesterday I saw a notice in our surgery in Tywyn saying a farmer had lost his Jack Russell. I wouldn't have thought any more about it, but there was a picture, and it was definitely Tincian. So I had no choice but to contact the owner.'

'Why didn't you pretend you hadn't seen it?' I asked him angrily.

'Because I'm a vet, and people put their trust in me. The owner isn't one of our clients, and I don't know the farm, but

I've explained the situation, and he's coming to my house tomorrow to pick up the dog.'

'No! No!' I shrieked, as if I had been stabbed, and gathered Chinks close to me.

Mrs Jones came running up the stairs and burst into the room, 'What on earth's going on?' she shouted. Siriol spoke to her quietly in Welsh and she went away again.

'Can I keep him until after school tomorrow?' I asked Gwennol.

'I should think so. It might be best if your Mum brings Tincian in the car Joel. And I'm sure I'll be able to find you a puppy just like him before long.'

The tears came then, 'I don't want a puppy. I only want Chinks,' I sobbed.

Siriol put a hand on my shoulder and patted.

Chinks was disturbed by my reaction, he pressed himself close to my legs and tried to wag his tail, rolling onto his back in the submission pose, and looking up at me with huge sad eyes. He just wanted everything to be normal again, and for us to be together always. Which is exactly what I wanted too.

I can't really describe our last night. It was too painful.

Mum did everything to try and help, she made me hot chocolate with a real chocolate flake to dip in, came into my room and sat on my bed chatting to me. She promised a puppy, a kitten, anything I wanted. I reckon if I'd asked for an iPod at that moment, I could have had one.

But I truly felt that she could drop every camera-phone, MP3 player and iPod ever made into the bottom of the lake at Talyllyn, and I wouldn't care. So long as I had Chinks next to me.

He's the first real thing who has loved me, and who I

132

have loved back. Except Mum, who doesn't count, because she's always been there.

It wouldn't have been half so bad if I'd had a Dad. Or a brother. But in a few short days, Chinks has made up for all the things I've never had.

'We'll go on holiday this summer. I'll find a way,' Mum promised.

I didn't want a holiday. Unless Chinks was there to run along the beach with me.

'And Gramps is coming in just over a week, and he could help you choose a puppy.'

I didn't want a puppy. Why couldn't she see this?

A sudden hope flickered in my chest, 'Could you ask the farmer if he would swap Chinks, and we could give him a puppy instead?' I asked her.

'Chinks is an adult dog, he's probably been trained to catch mice and rats on the farm, and anyway, he doesn't belong to us.' She rubbed her eyes distractedly. 'It's my fault, I shouldn't have let you keep him. I should have seen this coming - It's the story of my life.'

Then she hugged me, squishing Chinks in-between our two bodies, 'Joel love, I'd give you the world if I could.'

'I don't want the world, I only want Chinks,' I replied.

School was horrendous next day. I didn't hear a single word in lessons, I didn't play footie at lunch break, and never spoke to Emrys all day. He understood.

Every minute I looked at my watch and thought, seven more hours 'til I have to lose Chinks…. six more hours… five more.

'It's bad,' Emrys said, flicking the strap on his school bag, 'It's too bad. You've only had him a few days.'

When we got off the bus, although my heart leaped to see Chinks straining at the lead, it also ached to know this was the very last time.

I cried all the way to Abergynolwyn in our car. It's not just my heart that's going to get broken, it's Chinks' heart too. He feels the same way as me. He knows he's always been meant for me. Like the two rocks in the Isles of Scilly that I told you about, so close together in the water they're nearly touching.

And I'd been right believing that when I found my dog, we'd be like the two rocks. Two halves of a whole. Meant to be together.

When we pulled into Gwennol's drive there was a beat-up green Landrover parked already. I knew what that meant.

'I think it would be best if you said goodbye to Chinks here love,' Mum persuaded. 'I'll take him in. it will be far worse if you have to hand him over to the owner yourself.'

The cry that came out of me didn't sound anything like my normal voice. It was more like the howl of an animal. Chinks put his paws on my shoulders and licked my face frantically. I tried to hold on to him, stretching my arms out

134

and fighting Mum as she pulled him out of my arms.

Mum was sobbing as she tugged Chinks away from me, then the car door slammed shut and I saw Chinks for the last time, he was looking over his shoulder and his eyes seemed to be calling 'Joel!'

I was vaguely aware of a strange man looking at me from Gwennol's door. Then I saw nothing else but my knees and tear-soaked fingers in front of my face.

Several minutes passed before Mum came back. She didn't speak, but she had Chinks' collar and lead in her hand. Her face was red and streaked with tears.

She cried all the way home, and kept saying, 'I'm sorry Joel, I'm so sorry,' through her tears.

When we reached the cottage I found an envelope pushed under the mat. It had my name on it.

Dear Joel
I am so glad you came to live here, and I am so sorry about Chinks because I loved him too and I know you loved him much, much more.

When you are really sad it might be good to think about Chiclet's eggs which may hatch into chicks, and about the summer when we can go in the sea at Aberdyfi.

But when you are too sad to think about anything, then I'll come round and try to cheer you up.

From your freind Siriol

I'm not sure why, but Siriol's note made me cry even more.

As I sat eating pizza and chips (my favourite supper, Mum was being really nice,) I kept imagining Chinks' broken heart, and his little face staring out of the back of a beat-up Landrover. He would be watching out for me wherever he went.

'We'll go into Shrewsbury at the weekend and buy you a new England shirt,' Mum said.

'Any one you want, Gramps is sending money for it. So you can have the best.'

'Thanks,' I said, knowing I can't take an England shirt for a walk, or see it running towards me when I get off Morgan's bus.

'I thought we could play a game tonight, but I reckon your heart wouldn't be in it, and the TV won't distract you either. So can I tell you a story?' Mum asked.

'As long as it isn't about a dog,' I said. How could a story help? I hoped she wouldn't start reading out of a book. But I was so empty and wrung out that I hadn't got the energy to argue or resist. I settled back into the cushions limply.

Mum poured herself a cup of tea, smoothed her hair, picked invisible bits from her jumper, and began.

'All the best stories start the same way,' she said, 'So here goes. Once upon a time there was a kid called Seren who grew up on a tough estate. She was a bit like Siriol – sassy, honest and friendly. But she never had any money for the things other kids had, like bikes and fashionable clothes.

'Her parents were strict but fair, and there was no chance of her growing up spoilt, because although she was an only child, there wasn't any money to spoil her with.

'She made friends with girls and lads, and she was clever

- her teachers said she was bright enough to be a doctor or a vet, which is what she really wanted because she loved animals, but nobody from her estate had ever been to university, never mind become a vet.

'She left school at sixteen and went to work in the local supermarket. And although she wished she could carry on studying, she knew her dream could never come true, and that her life would work out OK, because she had her friends around her.

'And it probably would have been OK, if the *Terrible Thing* hadn't happened to her. The *Terrible Thing* was caused by her boss at the supermarket. No-one knew it at the time, but he was taking money out of the till, and putting it in his pocket, and fixing the figures so no-one could tell the money was missing. Until one day an auditor came into the store from Head Office posing as a shopper. The auditor bought his purchases and paid for them with a twenty pound note that he had secretly marked.

'After the store closed that night, the auditor revealed his identity, and went through the till. His twenty pound note was missing. Something made Seren suspect her boss, but she didn't say anything, because who would believe that the manager was a thief? She had been working on the till during that day, and her boss accused her of stealing the money.

'She denied it of course, but before she went home, her boss insisted that the auditor searched her purse. Seren had nothing to hide, and handed over her bag.

'Imagine her shock and horror when the auditor pulled out the very twenty pound note that had gone missing.

'She was fired that night, and her boss spoke to the local newspaper about the story, so after that, Seren couldn't get a job anywhere in the area.

'Her family didn't have enough money to pay a good solicitor to defend her case, and Seren ended up in court, being tried for theft. Her boss produced pages of figures showing that money had been disappearing since she began to work at the store. Seren was sent to prison for a few months, and after her release she had lost all her confidence, and felt she had no future.

'Her parents moved house so she could rebuild her life in a new area, but Seren was too unhappy to go out or make friends.

'Twelve years passed and Seren was now twenty-eight. She hadn't had a boyfriend since she was fifteen. This was a real problem, because Seren loved kids. She loved kids, babies and toddlers. All of them, even the screaming dribbling ones. Her only happy times were the days when her younger cousins came to visit, and she played Lego, Scrabble or Cowboys and Indians with them.

'She talked to her parents about this, and after a lot of thinking, she went to see her Doctor to ask about having a baby.

'It wasn't going to be easy to have a baby on her own, but Seren decided to take this one chance of having the only thing in the world she really wanted - somebody to love, and to love her back. A bit like you and Chinks in fact.

'Everything went well, and nine months later, Seren gave birth to a bouncing baby daughter. Her little girl brought joy into her life, and eventually Seren was well enough to get another job, and she and her beautiful girl lived happily ever after.'

Mum put down her mug - the tea had gone cold while she had been talking.

'It's you, isn't it?' I asked her. 'It's your story.'

'Perhaps. Some of it. But enough of my story to explain why you haven't got a Dad. That part is true. I know I've always said you haven't got a Dad, because I believed that was the simplest way of explaining when you were small. The details were far too complicated to talk about.'

'Tell me about my Dad.'

'I can't Joel, not at the moment. I've told you a story to explain as much as I can. All I can say right now is that he was white, he'd been to university, and he had brown hair and blue eyes. That will have to satisfy you for now.'

'It's not enough.'

'No, I've begun to understand that in the past few days, since Gwennol told me off. But in reality, you *don't* have a Dad. Because being a father isn't a case of biology, it's being there, through thick and thin. I couldn't give you that kind of Dad, because... well, the story explains some of the reasons.'

I had so much to take in that I didn't reply.

Mum went on, 'Whenever you asked me about your father, I felt really angry inside, and defensive. I blamed you for asking the question, and thought I should be enough for you. That you shouldn't need a man in your life, or anyone but me. After all, it was me that brought you up. But Gwennol talked some sense into me the other day. Maybe it's easier for him to see what's important, because he hasn't got long left... to live. But I'm sorry Joel, sorry that it's taken me fourteen years to say all this.'

'Why did you need to have a baby? Why didn't you just get a job as a teacher or something, or be a child-minder. Then you would have seen lots of kids?'

'Because I wanted a child of my own, that was biologically mine, and I wanted to be pregnant, all of that.'

'That's selfish, when you hadn't got a husband. In the

olden days you'd have had to go without, before they invented adoption and test tube babies.'

She didn't reply.

'Would you be mad if I said I'd like to find my Dad?' I asked quietly.

She looked calm, and sad, 'I'm afraid that isn't possible Jo-Jo.'

'I don't believe you, someone must be able to help us find him.'

'I don't have any way of finding him, or getting in touch. Nor do Gran-Wen or Gramps, or the doctors and nurses at the hospital where you were born. That's the way it is, and there's no law saying we have to be able to trace him.'

'Well that's wrong. Bad and wrong,' I replied angrily, 'and the people who made that law obviously weren't children without Dads. Because any idiot - any brain-dead idiot could tell you that every child wants to have a Mum and a Dad.'

Mum looked wounded, 'Not every child would feel like you Joel.'

'That's rubbish, EVERY child would. Every child whose parents are divorced, or dead, or...... adopted or made in a test tube, or cloned. Or even Jesus!' I was yelling now.

'What's Jesus got to do with it?' Mum asked helplessly.

'And you forced me to be born, even though I never asked for it, and even though you couldn't give me a proper family, and then you made me give back the only thing I ever loved in my whole life, and I wish I had cancer like Gwennol...,' I couldn't finish because the words turned into the animal howl, like the one that had come out of me in the car when Mum was taking Chinks away.

Mum took me in her arms and cradled me, as if I were a little baby.

I must have fallen asleep, because when I woke the fire had gone out, Mum was still holding me, and my watch said two am.

There was so much going round in my head. Chinks, my missing Dad, and now the awful news that Mum had been accused of a crime she didn't commit.

I wanted to talk about some of this, and so I had a chat with Emrys at school. A man to man chat.

'Do you get on with your Dad?' I asked him, as we sat on the steps outside the Science block at break.

'Pretty much, yeah.'

'I found out last night I'll never be able to trace my Dad.'

'Oh.'

'He could be anyone, he might be Jonny Wilkinson.'

'Cool. Or Mickey Rooney.'

I pulled a face.

'P'raps not,' Emrys grinned.

The chat I had with Siriol was different.

'You know that news item you taped for me?' I asked her after school. We were sitting in the hay barn just below Chicklet's nest, 'Well Mum says she can't get in contact with my biological Dad.'

Siriol raised her eyebrows and tipped her head.

'And I'll never be able to trace him. That's the law.'

'That's a stupid law.'

'Yeah.'

She leaned forward, 'They should make all biological Dads sign a form saying they will leave their address and phone number so their kid can contact them when they're older. It's so *ob*vious. Why don't they let people our age make laws? Then there wouldn't be any starving people in Africa, or global warming, and we'd all have piles of money because we'd get rid of taxes.'

'Exactly.'

'But there is one good thing,' she said thoughtfully, 'Your Mam must have wanted you really desperately. Otherwise she wouldn't have bothered. At least you know you weren't an accident. Any baby that's adopted or made in a test tube must be *to*tally wanted. I might be an accident, cos I'm an only child, and my parents don't really like each other much. They're always arguing. But your Mam wanted her own special baby, that was truly hers.'

'I hadn't thought of it like that,' I said.

'Shall we dam up the stream?'

'Yeah. Last one there's a turd.'

Siriol was a star that weekend. So was Mum to be honest. She took both of us into Shrewsbury, and we had lunch in a café, she bought me the new England shirt, and... can you believe this... an MP3 player! It was £59.99 in Argos, and Gramps had transferred the money into Mum's bank account to pay for it.

I saw four Jack Russell terriers in total. One in the town on a lead, and three on pavements that I spotted out of the car window. None of them was exactly like Chinks, but my stomach hurt every time.

And there are quite a few TV adverts starring dogs like Chinks at the moment. They seemed to be showing them on purpose over the weekend, just to spite me.

If anything really awful has ever happened to you, this next bit will make sense. If nothing awful has happened, then I hope it never will. There were moments of time – like when we were choosing the MP3 player – that I forgot about losing

Chinks for a few seconds. And then a bolt of hurt would hit me in the stomach and I remembered.

This happened every morning, as soon as I woke. First I would just open my eyes like normal, and realise it was morning, then – suddenly - the same pain would hit. Like a thump in a fight, the same winded feeling that left my stomach aching. And the memory of sitting in the car with Chinks saying goodbye would come flooding back.

Siriol seemed to know when I was having those painful moments, and every time I had one, she suggested a game, a video or a bike ride. It's funny really, when I lived in Staines if you'd asked me whether I'd ever have a mate who's a girl, I'd have said, 'Ha ha, you need your head testing!'

I was glad when Monday came again. School was a way of keeping my mind occupied, and in five days time, Gramps would be back for the weekend. And Mum said we would go and look at a couple of puppies that Gwennol knew about in Tywyn. I didn't want a puppy, but I was willing to go and have a look.

The sun was hot as we bounced home on Morgan's bus. I showed Emrys my MP3 player, and Siriol said we'd go for a dip in the stream.

As Siriol and I dragged our coats, bags, jumpers and school ties behind us along our track, I was thinking about Chinks, and dying for a cold drink.

We rounded the last bend at the farmhouse, and I looked up. Siriol had stopped dead in her tracks. There, ahead of us, and parked beside our cottage, was a 1989 red Peugeot 205.

My heart missed a beat and banged against my windpipe.

'No! it can't be!' Siriol whispered under her breath.

I dropped my coat, bag, jumper and slumped to the ground.

Over and over in my head went the words, 'No, no, it can't be him. Davey can't come back!'

'Stay here,' Siriol ordered. 'Don't move.'

She dropped her stuff and ran into our cottage. She was inside for two or three minutes, not more. When she re-appeared she looked furious.

'Follow me,' she said, 'and leave your stuff.'

She led me behind the farmhouse, through the trees and across the brook at a shallow crossing up-stream. Then she climbed into the woods on the other side. The trees became closer together, and the ground was damp.

'This is my secret place,' she said over her shoulder. 'No-one knows about it. OK?'

I nodded.

We had been walking for about fifteen minutes. The ground flattened in front of us, and at the far side of a small clearing, I saw a large rocky outcrop. Siriol led me behind it. I hadn't expected what I saw next, but someone had fixed up a proper den, with a black plastic roof, a flap of plastic animal feed bags as a door, and furniture inside. There were crates for chairs, a box, cups and books.

This is how much she trusts me - I thought - bringing me here.

'Right, sit down,' she said. 'Davey was there. I was very direct, and they know I'm not happy.'

I watched her burning eyes and pursed mouth, and could see that her anger must have been obvious.

'He was sitting on the sofa with your Mam. He had his arm round her, and she'd been crying. I said, 'What's he doing here?' and your Mam looked shocked by my bluntness.

'She told me Davey has come back because he was unhappy in Staines and he's realised he made a big mistake by leaving. She asked where you were and I said, 'Joel's not coming in while HE'S here.' I said 'HE' in a very meaningful way. You know, like 'He – the foul thing the cat dragged in that isn't fit to have a name."

I couldn't help smiling at her. She's amazing.

'Davey was grinning in a sort of cheesy, stupid way. If I have that look, Mam tells me to wipe the smile off my face.'

I could picture his expression perfectly.

'Your Mam said, 'This time it will be different. Davey knows he's got to accept Joel, and he's going to be a proper step-Dad. Please tell Joel that I want to speak to him, and tell him not to worry."

'Not to worry!' I shouted. 'What a stupid, pathetic thing to say! What am I going to do?'

Siriol produced two cartons of Ribena from a box. And two Kit-Kats. She sipped and munched while she thought, 'You can go home, or you can stay with me at the farmhouse. Or you can sleep here.'

'Thanks,' I said, and I meant it.

'At some point you'll have to go home, but I think you can lay the law down a bit. If Davey says he's going to be different, then he's got to prove it. And you can always leave home if he breaks his promise.'

'First Chinks, and now this,' I said feeling the sharp thump hit my stomach again, 'I don't think I can bear it.'

'It's going to be OK,' she replied, 'I know that inside.'

'Do you think we can find out where Chinks' owner lives and steal him back again? The farmer would just think he was lost.'

'But Uncle Gwennol would know.'

I knew the idea was hopeless as soon as I suggested it.

'Can I really stay with you at the farm?'

146

'Of course. Mam and Da are very chilled. They don't worry about things like visitors. Do you want me to ask them?'

I nodded and Siriol pulled her mobile out of her pocket. It had a signal – just.

She spoke in Welsh, and I actually caught a few of the words – impressing myself because I've only been learning the language for a few days.

She decked the call and explained, 'Mam says she'll need to ask your Mam, just to make sure. She says the spare bed's made up.'

'But Mum's bound to say no. Then I'll have to stay here in your den,' I said, feeling a bit worried at the prospect. But I could live without ALL my home comforts if it meant I was escaping Davey.

I chewed the last mouthful of biscuit while I thought things through.

Siriol's phone rang and she spoke in Welsh again, then translated for me, 'Mam says we should go back and talk about it, she's going to have a chat with your Mam now.'

'I know!' I yelled, suddenly struck with a brilliant plan, 'I could ask Gwennol if I could stay with him in Abergynolwyn!'

Siriol looked at her phone, 'You got any credit?'

'Yeah, loads.'

'Boys always have credit,' she said, holding out her hand for my phone, 'Cos you never communicate.'

She rang Gwennol from my handset and said in English, 'Can Joel come and stay with you please, because his step-dad from hell has come back.' Then she handed the phone back to me to carry on the conversation.

'So what's the trouble mate?' Gwennol asked me.

'Mum's boyfriend's back.'

'Is that so bad?'

'It's terminal. He threw a chair at Mum, he hates me, and I can't live with him.'

'But your Mum can't live without you. That would be impossible for her.'

'Then she's got to choose. Me or him.'

'Have you talked to her?'

'There's no point.'

'Well I tell you what, I'll ring you back later when you've spoken to her. Is this your mobile number?'

'Yeah,' I said, knowing that once the adults started talking to each another, the chance of a sensible outcome was over. Adults never understand how you're feeling, and they force their bad decisions on to you. I saw a programme on TV recently where two parents decided to sell up and move to Switzerland to run a B&B in a ski resort. They never even considered the feelings of their two teenage kids. The kids were so miserable, they'd lost everything and hated Switzerland. Adults are so selfish.

I said goodbye to Gwennol and rang off.

'I'll just stay here for the moment,' I said, 'if that's OK.'

'Course,' Siriol replied, 'I'll fetch you some supper when I come back later. And I'll let you know what's going on.'

At first I was quite happy on my own. I explored a bit, ate another biscuit, and played a few games on my phone. Then I began to get lonely. And started to imagine what it would be like in the woods if I had Chinks with me. He would have sniffed all around the den, licked the biscuit wrappers, and then fallen asleep on my knee. I would have been so content and safe, and after I had thought about that, I felt completely desperate. If Davey had come back to live with Mum, then my life wasn't worth living any more.

My watch said 18.10, and I was starving. The warm spring day had cooled down, and I hadn't got my jumper or coat, so I was going to be really cold out here in the woods. I also knew that once darkness fell, I would be scared stiff. I wished I hadn't watched *Doctor Who* on Saturday night. That was bound to make me terrified once the daylight faded.

Then I noticed the charge on my phone was down to one blip. So I wouldn't even be able to call for help.

Just then I heard footsteps in the dead leaves outside. I stayed in hiding, and was relieved when Siriol pulled open the door-flaps and came in beside me. She had my coat.

'Thanks,' I said pulling it on for warmth.

She handed me a cheese sandwich and a banana, which I devoured straight away while she talked.

'Some good news and some not so good,' she began. 'When I got back, your Mam was in my kitchen talking to my Mam. No sign of Davey, thankfully. They asked about you straight away, and I said you weren't going home. It was really difficult to come back here without them following me. I cycled towards the lake, then abandoned the bike and walked from there. They didn't see where I went.

'Apparently, Davey says he's back for good, but as he's told that story before, I wouldn't assume it's definite. Your Mam is worried sick about you, and she kept on saying that Davey's made loads of promises and knows he's got to be nice to you.'

'Or what?' I said, my mouth full of sandwich.

'I dunno. But your Mam seemed different compared to when Davey left. More sure of herself, tougher. She said you could stay at the farmhouse with me for tonight, that's the good news.'

'Then what?'

'She said after that, she would see.'

'Which means I have to go home.'

'You can come back here at any time. And we could make it a bit more homely, bring up a sleeping bag, blankets, proper food and stuff.'

I didn't tell her that I'd be too scared to spend the night in the den on my own.

'I'll come home with you for tonight then,' I said.

'You can ride on the back of my bike,' she offered, and that's what we did. It was a long walk to the bike, and a long uncomfortable cycle home afterwards.

I went straight into Siriol's kitchen instead of my cottage.

'It's good to see you Joel,' her Mum said, 'I'll go and tell your Mam you're here.'

She burst in and knelt beside me at the kitchen table, looking upset and worried.

'I'm not coming home,' I said flatly.

'Not tonight, no,' she replied.

'Or tomorrow. If HE's there.'

Mum put her head in her hands. 'Don't do this to me Joel, don't make me choose,' she said quietly.

Siriol interrupted, 'Mrs Tillyard, shall I fetch Joel's things?'

There was a knock at the farmhouse door. I looked up and saw Davey's orange ugly face staring sheepishly into the kitchen.

'There's a guy to see you,' he said to my Mum. Then he saw me and made a sort of humph. If it was meant to be a 'hello' then it was a pathetic attempt.

Uncle Gwennol appeared behind Davey and stepped inside.

Just for a moment no-one spoke or moved. Siriol, her Mam, me, Mum, Gwennol and Davey. No-one seemed to know what to do or say.

Davey obviously couldn't stand the pressure, because he vanished. Mum stood up, Gwennol shook her hand and Siriol offered us all a cup of tea.

Gwennol spoke first, to Mum, 'Dave seemed a bit miffed when I asked for you Caitlin, so you may need to reassure him I'm not your new man!'

I noticed Siriol's Mam shaking her head quietly.

Mum laughed in an embarrassed kind of way and sat at the table.

'Now - I have a suggestion,' Gwennol began, 'and it may be for a short time, or a slightly longer one.'

We were all looking at him, waiting for a way forward.

'If you agree Caitlin, then Joel can come and stay with me. It would make sense, especially at the moment, while he's looking for a puppy. The school bus stops in my village, I've got two spare bedrooms upstairs, and – frankly, I'd enjoy the company.' He smiled at me. 'I know more than most people about living with difficulties Joel.'

I guessed he meant the cancer.

Mum looked pleased and relieved in a way, 'You're very kind Gwennol, as long as it's only... temporary.'

'A stop-gap, until things settle down.' He looked pale and tired.

'Could I... I mean...' Mum stammered.

'Come and visit him? How about a cup of tea after school every day?'

'Thank you,' she said with relief, then a shadow passed

across her thin face, 'And I'm so sorry about all of this, I seem to have brought nothing but trouble into your lives,' she faltered.

'It's really exciting having you here,' Siriol enthused. 'Until you **Eng**lish came, nothing ever happened. We love it!'

All the adults laughed.

It was decided that I should go to Gwennol's straight away. Mum fetched my bag, packed with school books, towel, the stuff I'd dumped in the lane hours earlier, and a few of my essentials, like the MP3 player.

I hadn't got the slightest doubt about getting away from Davey at the cottage, and although I would miss Mum, nothing would have made me sleep in the next room to HIM again.

We bounced down the track in Gwennol's van. He was easy to be with, he doesn't talk all the time like some adults, and it's OK not to chat if you don't want to. For me, this was one of those times.

I had a choice of bedroom, and Gwennol sent me upstairs to pick one. There was a small single room facing the street, and a double at the back looking into the trees close to the railway line. I chose that room, because I loved the view, and there was plenty of space for a dog bed.

Gwennol called me downstairs for a cocoa.

'Tomorrow I'll fix you up with a TV and a video.'

'Wow, thanks,' I said, 'I haven't got a video in my room at Mum's.'

'It's a big day for me tomorrow,' he went on, 'I've got an appointment at the hospital in Dolgellau, to get the results of my monthly tests. I never look forward to those.'

'What's wrong with you exactly?' I asked.

'I had a tumour removed two years ago, and I've had no end of treatment since. But a few months ago it seemed to be coming back. Cancer's a tricky thing, but I think I've got a few more years left in me yet.'

'Is that why you're always tired?'

'That's the effect of the treatment, yes. And I refuse to do what I'm told, to give up work completely and rest. My job is what keeps me going, I love it.'

'Did you always want to be a vet?'

'Since I was five or six.'

'My Mum wanted to be a vet when she was little - I only just found that out.'

Gwennol looked shocked, and fascinated at the same time, 'Really? What made her change her mind?'

I told him the story of Seren and the terrible boss at the supermarket. He looked completely horrified as I talked about the prison part.

When I finished, he said, 'That's the kind of thing you see on the news, it's shocking, and no wonder your Mum didn't fancy the idea of getting married after an experience like that.' He stared into space, and I could tell he was really struck by what I'd told him.

'Do you think I could be a vet when I leave school?' I asked.

'Would you like to be?'

'Until I met you, I never thought I'd be able to do a job like that, but animals are the best thing in my life. I want to be able to clip chicken's wings like Siriol can, and give vaccinations, like you did to.....'

Gwennol nodded, so I wouldn't need to say Chinks' name out loud.

'Well how about you come with me tomorrow evening on a farm visit?'

I nodded enthusiastically.

'I could do with a fit assistant to carry my case and help me out. And there just might be a few puppies to look at too.'

I lay in bed in my new room and thought about all Gwennol had said, picturing myself giving injections and delivering lambs. The double bed was soft and warm, and the sound of a grandfather clock downstairs comforted me, ticking steadily like the beating heart of a real home.

At first it was weird getting on the school bus at a new stop. Siriol bounced out of her seat to ask if I was OK. None of the kids tease me about having a mate who's a girl, they're much more friendly than teenagers in Staines. And Emrys had saved my seat. I told him all about being a vet's assistant.

'That's cool,' he said, 'So are you getting a puppy or what?'

'Dunno,' I said, 'It's not a puppy I want.'

'I know, a puppy wouldn't be Chinks would it?'

When I got home to Gwennol, he was already packing the van, 'Your Mum's coming for supper, when we've finished our call. In fact she's *bringing* the supper, which is even better!'

The farm was beyond Talyllyn lake which looked stunning in the afternoon light. This time we approached from the west, and the expanse of water was smooth and dark, ringed by the steep hills on both sides. A few black and white ducks were dabbling at the edge, and a lone man was pulling a rowing boat out of the water by the hotel.

'What are you thinking?' Gwennol asked me.

I tried to find the right words, 'That it's like a film, but... more real. When I'm here I can't believe that London, power stations and motorways exist. And I feel as if they shouldn't. This is how all lakes ought to be.'

I wondered if that made sense.

'When I moved here from Cardiff I felt exactly the same,' Gwennol replied, 'As if I was suddenly living in a dream, no... living in heaven. Because if I was creating a lake and a

156

valley, with mountains and all, I'd be pretty chuffed if I'd designed this.'

In my chest I had the first feeling of happiness I'd had since Chinks left. A small happiness, but it was a start.

The farm looked like all the others I'd seen, grey, squat and snug. I carried the veterinary case, and Gwennol told me we would blood test one of the sheepdogs. It was in a kennel behind the house, and the farmer came out to greet us in his cloth cap and wellies, calling '*Croeso!*'

'Watch the dog, he's not keen on strangers,' Gwennol warned me. But the farmer muzzled the collie which meant I would be able to help.

'He's an old boy,' Gwennol explained as he examined the dog all over, 'but the client wants him to father one more litter. We'll take a blood test to find out what the trouble is.'

He held the dog's front leg and taught me how to shave the fur with a special electric razor. Then he took the blood sample. I was fascinated, and he praised me for keeping the dog under good control.

The farmer spoke and I heard the words *ci bach* which I remembered meant puppy. My feelings were mixed, wanting to see the puppies, but not necessarily to have one.

'Come and look at the litter Joel,' Gwennol said as he packed away the syringe and sample. 'They're collies, sired by this dog.'

The farmer led us into his back kitchen, which was a mess, and beside the boiler was a flat wooden crate containing an old blanket, a sleepy collie bitch, and six new-born puppies. Their eyes were still stuck shut, and they looked like small black and white barrels with stumpy legs.

'Two days old,' Gwennol said to me, checking them over quickly. The mother growled, but hadn't got the energy to do worse.

'Have you got homes for all these?' Gwennol asked, and the farmer replied in Welsh.

On the way home Gwennol told me three of the pups were sold, and that I could have one for fifty pounds.

'Fifty pounds!' I said. 'Maybe I'll just wait a while.'

'There will always be other litters round here, so no hurry.'

As we rounded the bend in Abergynolwyn and pulled into Gwennol's drive, my heart missed a beat, and the bottom dropped right out of my stomach. On the verge was parked a vehicle which I would recognise anywhere. It was the beat-up green Landrover.

'Oh no!' Gwennol said with feeling, 'That's bad timing. Sorry Joel.'

In the driver's seat sat the man I had already seen, and with his paws up on the passenger window and looking at us, was my Chinks, the real, the one, the only dog in the world for me.

The pain in my chest was now twenty times worse than it had been at any other time since I lost him, and Chinks began to bark and leap about in the Landrover as he recognised me.

Gwennol looked absolutely gutted, 'I don't know what's best Joel, do you think you should come in, or wait here? There's obviously something wrong with Chinks, or one of the owner's animals. He hasn't made an appointment.'

But I couldn't reply, just jumped out of the van and ran to the Landrover, pressing my palms against Chinks' window, the hot tears running down my cheeks.

All I wanted in the whole world was to touch the soft fur, and breathe in the scent of those velvety ears.

The farmer jumped out of his door, and there was a conversation between the men that I couldn't hear.

Meanwhile, Chinks was going frantic in the vehicle.

Then, 'Why don't you let him out?' Gwennol shouted to me, 'Don't you want to hold your very own dog!'

You're probably thinking this is the end of my story, and I honestly wish you were right.

It was without doubt the best evening of my life. While I was still hugging and stroking Chinks, Mum pulled up too. She couldn't believe her eyes.

Like Gwennol, at first she panicked, saying, 'Oh no! This will make things worse!' but I was laughing and reassuring her, 'It's OK, Chinks is mine! Gwennol says he's my dog!'

A moment later, the man shook my hand and got into his Landrover, saying, 'Look after each other!' and Mum and I rushed to Gwennol, both speaking at once, 'What happened?... Why has he brought Chinks back?'

'Hold on you two, let me get the door open,' Gwennol laughed.

I was so glad Mum was there to share this perfect moment.

Chinks bounced up and down for joy, and Mum seemed almost as pleased to see him as I was.

'Mr Meredith said he couldn't forget your broken face on the day you brought Chinks here Joel, and he said he can do without the dog perfectly well. He has two other dogs, and his wife never liked Chinks because of his bark.

'Thank you God! Thank you!' I said aloud, adding in my head thanks that Chinks has the kind of bark that annoys farmers' wives.

'Is it for ever?' I asked.

'And always. He's your dog Joel. Looks like you were right when you said you were meant to be together.'

That's when Mum started sobbing. Weird really, this was

the time to be happy, not sad. She plonked herself down at Gwennol's table and dropped her head into her hands. She cried for ages.

Gwennol didn't seem embarrassed, he rubbed Mum's shoulder and made her a cup of tea.

'Life eh!' he said, as she blew her nose.

'Sorry,' she sniffed, 'I'm just so happy for you Joel, and missing you, and wishing you and Davey could get on.'

'Things will be a whole lot better now you've got Chinks back won't they?' Gwennol asked me.

'Yup,' I said confidently.

It was the best supper on the best evening of my life. Chinks sat by my feet all the way through, and I stroked him every few seconds. Mum had brought Tuna Pasta Bake, and Apple Crumble with custard. Gwennol said if he ate another thing, he would rupture his stomach.

'How were your tests?' I asked, suddenly remembering.

'Not great news to be honest, but they'll increase the treatment, and, we'll see what next month brings. A bit of a relapse,' he explained to Mum.

'I'm sorry,' she said. 'Is it prostate?'

'Bowel,' he replied.

'Ah.'

'Joel told me you wanted to be a vet once.'

'That was a long time ago. Life kind of got in the way.'

'Joel did explain a little bit about the past. And I'm very sorry about what you went through.'

'But you managed it - became a vet I mean.'

'Well yes, but look what I had to sacrifice. This job doesn't fit well with family life, as you can see by the distinct lack of wives, fiancées - females in general round here!'

Mum laughed, and I stroked Chinks.

'But perhaps it's all for the best, because of my illness. It would have been dreadful if I'd had a wife and children.'

'Have you got any funny stories?' I asked Gwennol, 'about being a vet, like the ones in *All Creatures Great and Small*.'

'Well as a matter of fact I have. Which one do you want to hear, the world's fastest whippet, the biting hamster, or the talking budgie?'

'The whippet please,' I said, leaning forward on the table expectantly.

Mum looked peaceful and happy.

'Well, it all happened a long time ago, almost twenty years ago, when I was a student vet. Students have to 'see practice' while they're still learning, and they're allowed to do the simple things like injections, and very basic operations. Towards the end of my degree, I saw practice in a smart surgery in Swansea and, as I was almost qualified, the senior vet gave me more and more responsibility.

'One day an elderly couple came into the surgery with their equally elderly whippet. It was a sweet dog, and they loved it to pieces. I took the consultation and examined the dog, and was convinced it hadn't got long to live.

'The owners couldn't bear the thought of it suffering, and asked me if I would put it to sleep. As I was so young and inexperienced, I didn't want to do it while they were watching, because I wasn't very confident, and I politely suggested they should go home and leave their dog in my care.'

I interrupted, 'I thought you said this was a funny story?'

'Hang on until the end,' Gwennol went on, 'So the couple left in tears, and I felt wretched, as this was one of the first animals I'd ever put to sleep. While I prepared the injection, I turned my back and left the dog on the table. He was weak and calm, and I thought I could manage the job without the help of a nurse. As I turned my back, I didn't realise that when the owners had left the room, they hadn't closed the door of the consulting room behind them, and it had now swung wide open on its hinges.

'I turned back to the table, a full syringe in my hand, to carry out the sad task. But the whippet wasn't there. He had jumped off the table, run into the waiting room, and out of the building through the front door, which by chance was also open.

'Dropping the needle, I ran, out of the surgery, through the car park, and up the road. The whippet was ahead of me, but still in sight.

'I was younger and fitter then, but boy could that dog run! Up the main road, left at the lights, into a tree-lined avenue, round several bends, always ahead of me, but just in sight. He ran, and I chased for a full ten minutes, until the muscles in my legs were burning with exhaustion. Finally, I lost sight of him, and admitted to myself that I would never find the whippet. As I retraced my steps to the surgery, I felt like weeping, and knew I'd never deserve to qualify after such a dreadful mistake. And I didn't know what to say to my boss, or to the poor owners, who thought their pet was now at peace.'

Mum's eyes were as wide as eggcups as she listened to Gwennol's story.

'As I walked through the door of the surgery, a nurse rushed up and beckoned me into the staff kitchen, 'Gwennol, guess what? The owners of that whippet have been on the phone.'

'I hung my head in shame.

'The nurse went on, 'When they arrived home a few minutes ago, they couldn't believe their eyes, because their dog was waiting for them on the front step, and can you believe it? He was looking better than he has done for years. He'd run all the way home!'

'Moments later I was called to the phone and the whippet's owner was on the line, 'I just wanted to thank you,' he said to me, 'For giving us Ben back. It's an answer to prayer, and you've made our day!'

'And that whippet lived for another two years.'

Mum burst out laughing.

'It taught me to think very carefully before agreeing to put an animal to sleep, and most of all – when you're examining a dog, remember to shut the door!'

I pictured Gwennol, legging it down a road, chasing the streamlined Ben, and then I pictured the joy on the faces of the elderly couple. I grinned, smiled and giggled.

'I can't remember an evening when I had such fun,' Mum laughed, 'Thank you Gwennol, for having Joël, and for... everything.'

'Another coffee?' he asked, just as there was a thudding at the front door.

He answered, and I heard Davey's menacing voice in the hall, 'Caitlin!' he demanded.

'Oh, doesn't this look cosy!' he said sarcastically, as he came into the room, 'What a fine old time you're all having here!'

Chinks growled quietly in the back of his throat.

'Ruddy dog!' Davey snarled, 'Keep him away from me.'

He pulled Mum's arm roughly, and she looked completely embarrassed. She gave me a quick peck on the cheek and said a hasty goodnight, as Davey man-handled her out of the house.

'I see what you mean about him,' Gwennol said, putting

his arm round my shoulder. 'You OK?'

I didn't reply.

'In all my years, I've never met such a…. plonker,' he said. 'What a mess.'

Chinks jumped on to my lap to comfort me and I kissed his ears.

'You can stay here as long as you need to Joel. I've fixed up the video, and bought some decent breakfast cereals. And chin up, you've got your very own dog back.'

*F*or the next three weeks I stayed at Gwennol's. Mum came over most afternoons, and took me out. I figured Davey didn't want her to have any more cosy evenings in Gwennol's house with me.

We went to the coast, and to the café in Abergynolwyn, and took Chinks on walks up Bird Rock, to the quarry, and along the stream. Most times Siriol came too. Everything was great at Gwennol's, I'd have preferred to live with Mum obviously, but now Davey was back, that wasn't an option.

On the third Monday morning, I was eating breakfast with Gwennol, when he suddenly said, 'Hold out your hand Joel, the right one.'

I stretched out the wrist and Gwennol ran his finger over the underside, 'Does this hurt?' he asked, in his veterinary voice.

'Not really, only when I write loads in one go at school.'

The hard lump under the skin had been there for several weeks, but it had been getting more tender recently. It was the size of a small marble.

'It's a ganglion,' he explained, 'completely harmless, but it can get quite sore. I'll tell your Mum to make you an appointment at the doctor's. Most of them go away by themselves, but you should have it checked out.'

'OK,' I said, knowing this is one of the areas of life that adults take care of, not something I'd have a choice about. I nuzzled Chinks' head and snuffled his ear.

They didn't waste much time. When I got off the bus, Mum was waiting for me in her car.

'We've got an appointment in Tywyn,' she said, 'At four

o'clock.'

'Where's Chinks?' I asked, 'is he with Gwennol?'

'No. He spent the day at Siriol's, but just as I was leaving, Davey offered to take him for a walk. I thought that would be far nicer for Chinks than sitting in the car waiting for us in Tywyn.'

'You let Davey take him?' I asked.

'It'll do him good, get him used to Chinks, for... when you come home.'

I wasn't coming home, but I didn't say it just then.

'Poor Chinks,' was all I said, and I had a terrible worry at the back of my mind, 'Davey hates dogs.'

'He's changed,' Mum reassured me, and he's trying so hard Jo-Jo. Last week he bought me flowers, and he's fixing up a mini-gym at the cottage. The amount of work he's done is amazing, he's slow, but a perfectionist. The kitchen's finished, and the bathroom.' She paused for a moment, 'I want you to come home Joel, we could start with a family meal tonight, and take it from there.

'We're not a family,' I said.

'I've talked it over with Davey, and told him you'll come back for a trial period, you and Chinks obviously.'

My stomach was churning all the way to the doctors. I kept picturing Davey with Chinks, and convincing myself that he would hit him with a stick, or drag him roughly on the lead. I couldn't wait to get home and have Chinks safe with me.

The GP was a woman, and she prodded my ganglion and offered to get it looked at by a specialist if I wanted to make an appointment. Or I could wait another month and see. Mum decided I could wait.

'I'll just pop into the bakery and get us a cake for later,'

Mum said as we came out into the sunshine.

'Please can we just go back,' I begged, 'I want to see Chinks.'

When our car pulled into the drive, Siriol ran straight out to me from the farmhouse, 'Surprise!' she called, and pulled me towards the farmyard.

The doves, startled as always, rose from the ground, circled, and landed on the barn roof.

'Look!' giggled Siriol, and I followed the direction of her pointing finger.

'Chicklet! She's got chicks!' I said, seeing my white hen, plump and sleek now, and surrounded by one, two, three, four fluffy yellow chicks. They had tiny stumpy wings, weeny beaks, and they were making a continuous cheeping sound, that made you want to rush over and protect them. They were absolutely gorgeous.

'You're a Dad!' Siriol laughed.

'Davey took Chinks for a walk, have you seen him?' I asked her.

'His car's not there. I'll come and wait with you,' she said.

We watched the chicks for a moment, they were following Chicklet and pretending to peck, huddling close to each other and to their Mum.

'Nature's amazing,' I said. 'They used to be eggs!'

'You're funny,' Siriol said.

There was no sign of Davey. We sat on the gate opposite our cottage and waited.

It wasn't long before the old red Peugeot appeared, far too fast along the lane as usual, and coming to a screeching halt. He got out, slammed the door and headed for the cottage. He was whistling, and there was no sign of Chinks.

'He probably dropped Chinks at Uncle Gwennol's,' Siriol said.

My heart began to beat too fast.

'Come with me,' I breathed, and sprinted into the kitchen. Davey had gone into the lounge.

'Where's Chinks?' I said, going right up to him, and standing inches away from his face.

'Ah, I've got some bad news,' he began. Mum came through, drying her hands on a tea towel.

'What bad news?' she asked gently.

Davey sidled to the window, trying to put some space between himself and me.

'Bad news, I don't know how to tell you both, very bad news. But I did all I could.'

'WHERE'S CHINKS?' I screamed, '**WHERE IS CHINKS**?' and I began to hit Davey on the arm, hit him frantically and fiercely, I wanted to kill him. He put his hands up to his face and I carried on punching his body.

Mum put herself between us, 'Joel, just control yourself! And Davey, tell us where the dog is.'

Siriol took my hand, it was a small gesture of support. I gripped it for dear life.

'I'll forgive your little outburst young man,' Davey said, 'which is most uncalled for, after all I've done for you this afternoon. I took the dog for a walk along the cliffs just south of Borth, lovely spot. He was having a smashing time, chasing the butterflies and all that.'

I bore into Davey with my eyes, hating him, murdering him in my head.

'And out of nowhere, some bloke fired a gun, or his car engine backfired, and there was an almighty cracking sound. I jumped out of my skin, and unfortunately, so did the dog.

Scared out of his wits he was. And I just didn't have time. My biggest regret is that I should have kept him on the lead. But he was so startled he ran for it, towards the cliff edge. That was the last I saw of him, right over the edge he went, and it's a fall of seventy feet into the sea if it's an inch.'

'Noooooooo!' I screamed, 'NO, NO, NO, NO!'

I threw myself on the ground and beat the rug with my fists, hitting my head on the slate floor.

'Stop it, stop it!' Mum screamed.

Davey was still speaking, 'There was nothing I could do, I looked for him of course, and called his name, and... at least he wouldn't have known anything about it.'

Mum grabbed my head between her hands and then I saw Siriol, who walked calmly up to Davey and smacked him in the face. One massive slap, with all the force of her body.

'Aaaaargh!' Davey yelled, and rushed to the stairs, holding his cheek.

'Get your car keys!' Siriol yelled at Mum, 'Quick!'

even though she was the youngest, Siriol took charge of the situation, took charge of Mum and of me. Neither of us had any idea what to do.

'Drive, to Aberdyfi, fast as you can,' Siriol urged. She was clear and calm. 'We can't reach Borth by road, it would take too long - we'd have to drive miles inland to get round the estuary.'

She was thinking on her feet, 'We'll go straight to the Coastguard, and just beg him to take us out by boat. Emrys' uncle works on the lifeboats, it'll all depend if they're busy.'

I couldn't focus on her instructions, or the plans, my mind filled with the horrendous image, a cliff twenty-five metres above the waves, rocks, cold water, and Chinks falling.

Mum passed her mobile to Siriol, 'Dial your uncle,' she said.

Up until now I've always nagged Mum about her driving. She's cautious, which is a polite way of saying she's rubbish. She sits on a cushion with her face almost touching the windscreen and drives at ten miles an hour. Or fifteen if we're in a rush. She never overtakes, and she always lets other drivers out.

Well this was a new Mum driving our car. She had her foot flat on the accelerator, and overtook every vehicle we caught up with, including a Series 3 BMW. I didn't know she had it in her, and our car must have been as shocked as I was.

'Come on! Come on!' she shouted all round the one-way system in Tywyn, almost knocking an old lady off her bike at the Sainsbury's turning, and cursing - loads. When we got

171

stuck behind a bus at the road-works, she slammed on her brakes, reversed, did a U-turn, took a detour round the housing estate and hit the open road into Aberdyfi at eighty-five miles an hour.

I was so proud of her.

'Uncle Gwennol's phoning ahead to the Coastguard,' Siriol said.

We passed the big hotel on the left and the sand-dunes on the right, the dunes where I had played so happily with Chinks only days ago.

'As soon as we get to town, pull into the surface car park on the right,' Siriol ordered. 'Park anywhere here - the Coastguard's in the lifeboat station next to the loos.'

We dumped the car and ran.

'You can't leave it there,' called a traffic warden.

'There's been an accident, on the cliffs,' Mum pleaded, 'it's an emergency.'

'I see, I see,' the warden replied. 'I'll put a special note on your car, just leave it with me, no problem.'

We were already out of earshot.

Siriol took complete charge. Inside the RNLI station an elderly man in a peaked hat was reading the paper behind a reception desk.

'My name's Siriol Jones from *Tynycornel Isaf.* Our dog has fallen off the cliffs south of Borth. We can't get there by road, can you take us to search for him by boat?'

The man put down his newspaper, 'Ah, your vet called and the Watch Officer has already gone out in the small launch.'

Behind the man was a control room full of electrical equipment, radios and sound systems. There was a constant stream of signals, and announcements going on.

172

'You'd better come through,' he said to us, lifting the flap that formed part of his desk. We walked through to the control room.

The man fiddled with dials and put headphones on. He spoke occasionally, using words like 'Roger, Come in, and Over,' like pilots do in the air.

'Where exactly did the dog fall?' he asked Mum.

'We're not sure, the cliffs south of Borth, that's all we know.'

'Hang on,' he said, listening to a radio message, 'Roger, understood.' Then he turned to us, 'Right, the station at Aberystwyth have launched an RIB, that's an inshore Rigid Inflatable Boat, which can go into shallow water, so there are two boats out there looking for your dog.'

'Is there any chance he'll survive?' Siriol said, asking the question I'd had on my lips since we first saw the coastguard.

'All depends. The current is very strong, and the water's cold at this time of year. Or he may have fallen onto rock, in which case, he wouldn't stand a chance. I'll show you,' he said, pointing to a large wall-map of the coastline.

'We're here,' his finger rested on Aberdyfi, set slightly east above the wide sandy estuary, 'and the cliffs are here,' his finger traced the coast south to Borth, Upper Borth, and the stretch of rocks lower down.

'There's a cliff rescue team on board the RIB, they have all the kit. So if your dog has fallen onto a rocky outcrop, and is stranded above the waterline, they'll be able to get him down.'

'If he's in the water, how long will he survive?' Siriol asked.

'Late April, not long, twenty or thirty minutes.'

I looked at my watch, and knew that Chinks must have

been lost more than an hour ago. Because Davey had already driven the long way back from Borth. It was much more than an hour.

Mum must have seen my face - she put her arm round me.

'Do you have a mobile?' the coastguard asked her. 'If you give me your number, you could go and get yourselves a hot drink in one of the tea-rooms. Probably better than waiting here on tenterhooks,' he said, nodding his head in my direction.

'Good idea,' she replied.

We re-parked the car, paid for a ticket, and walked aimlessly towards the row of shops and hotels that line the seafront. I wasn't at all hungry.

Mum sent us inside a tea-room, 'I'm just going to make a call,' she said, 'I won't be long.'

Siriol and I sat at the table in the window. The waitress took our order and we watched Mum on the pavement outside.

'She's phoning HIM,' Siriol said.

'I know.'

Mum looked very agitated, she kept gesturing with her free hand, and rubbing her fingers through her hair. Then she seemed to lose her temper, and we could hear her raised voice through the tea-room window.

'Why do you think he did it?' Siriol asked.

'Because Mum told him I was going back to live with them, for a trial period, with Chinks.'

'It wasn't an accident was it?'

'No.'

'Do you think he pushed him over the cliff?'

'All I know is that Chinks wouldn't fall off. Do you remember the day we went to Nant Gwernol, to the old quarry, and Chinks went right to the edge.'

'Yes.'

'And even though he set off a landslide of rocks, he didn't fall over, he was sure footed.'

'Yeah, I remember saying that day, dogs have a sixth sense of danger.'

'He's gone for good this time,' I said. There was no feeling inside me, no anger, no emotion of any kind. Just emptiness, a black hole where my heart should be.

Mum came inside and poured her tea.

'Joel, I'm going to be completely honest with you. That was Dave on the phone.'

Siriol and I looked at her intently, just listening and blinking.

'Deep down inside I can't believe that Davey has done anything to harm Chinks, BUT he does hate dogs. So I just asked him to tell me the honest truth about what happened. I love him, and I was prepared to believe him. He told me that Chinks was being disobedient and just jumped off the cliff edge.'

'But he said!' began Siriol.

Mum held up her hand, 'I know. Earlier he said Chinks was startled by a loud noise, like a gunshot. I've been asking myself whether anyone could be awful enough to hurt a dog, even one they didn't like. But perhaps the bit about the cliff didn't happen at all. Perhaps he actually took Chinks to the RSPCA, or just abandoned him somewhere, and made up the story about the walk.

'I've phoned Gwennol and asked him to contact all the local dog rescue centres just in case. And he'll put the word around.'

I spoke out of the emptiness that was in my stomach, 'This time I won't get him back. It can't happen twice.'

Mum said, 'You're wrong Joel, we're going to keep on hoping.'

I looked her full in the face and said flatly, 'I'll never be able to forgive you for this.'

Her face changed from worry to despair, 'Don't say that Joel, please don't say that.'

'Joel is only saying what he feels right now,' Siriol said.

Mum rubbed her eyes, 'All through February and March and April in 1979, I sat in a prison cell. Although I had never committed a crime, I was forced to suffer a criminal's punishment. I had enough time on my hands to dwell on the wrongs I'd suffered at the hands of my boss, the judge and the jury. My anger was so deep, I thought I could never forgive them. That anger took ten years of my life, far longer than the prison sentence. Hate Davey Joel, if you have to hate somebody, but try not to hate me.'

There was no point staying in the tea-room any longer.

We went back to the Coastguard for news.

'Nothing to report I'm afraid,' he said.

I said to the man, 'Please can you give them *my* mobile number, and ask them to phone *me* if there's any news. Good or bad,' I added.

He wrote the number down and underlined it.

It was a sorry journey back to Abergynolwyn that evening. Not one of us spoke, and you could actually feel the tension between Mum and me in the atmosphere.

Mum dropped me at Gwennol's. After I got out of the car I saw Mum break into tears, and Siriol put her arm round her.

I went inside, and noticed that our car was still parked on the kerb outside.

Gwennol didn't say a word. He came out of his sitting-cum-bedroom and held out his strong arms. He folded me against his chest and let me take out all my hurt and pain on him. I flailed my arms and he carried on holding me, tightly, firmly. Like a Dad would.

Ten minutes later there was a knock at the door. It was Mum.

'Joel, I want you to come with me. Not to stay, but to hear something very important. I want you to be there.'

I looked up at Gwennol for reassurance.

'I'll bring him in the van,' he said.

On the short journey back to our cottage, I told him what Mum had said about her phone conversation with Davey. And about survival times in an April sea.

'They'll be doing everything possible to find Chinks Joel. If anyone can find him, those guys will, they're the best,' Gwennol said. 'I have a feeling your Mum's going to say something to Davey, so it'll probably be best if I wait outside with Siriol.'

We parked, and Siriol took my place in her uncle's van.

I followed Mum into the cottage, and my heart started

to beat too fast again. It was partly the fear of Davey, and partly anticipation.

Mum dropped her keys on the kitchen floor, didn't bother to shut the front door, and marched slowly into the sitting room. She was a woman with a mission.

The TV was on, and Davey was asleep, an empty supper tray askew on his lap, six empty beer cans at his feet. He was snoring.

'Get up!' Mum said, in a low voice that seemed to come from the very pit of her stomach.

Davey opened his eyes and sat up slowly.

'Hello darling,' he drawled, 'and hello Joel.' It was the first and only time he has ever used my name.

'Get up!' Mum repeated.

Davey struggled to his feet. The sofa was between them, and I was behind Mum.

'There are no words black enough to describe you,' Mum said in the low, menacing voice. 'You are not a man, you are a worm. A lying, deceiving coward. And you're full of slime. You've slimed your way into my life, with your lies about love, false promises that you had left your wife. Slimy words to wriggle your way into my heart and my home.

'Well let me tell you,' she pointed, moving around the sofa and closing in on him, 'I realised today that I never loved you. Never. I let you in because I needed someone. But I don't need YOU! I love Joel, I love Chinks, and I love myself enough to know what's good for me.

'You have five minutes to get out of this house. And in five minutes and one second, I pick up the phone and call the police to tell them what you have done to our dog.'

Davey had pressed himself against the wall as Mum pierced him with her forefinger, 'I can't drive Caitlin, I've had too much to drink.'

'I don't care if you've had two bottles of whisky. I don't care if you have to walk to Staines from here. You just,' - each word was now accompanied by a sharp stab at his chest, 'Get your stuff and GET OUT!'

I didn't move, didn't breathe.

Everything had gone into slow-motion again. In slow-mo, Mum dropped her hand, Davey moved to the stairs, fetched his bag, coat and keys.

'It could all have been so different,' he pleaded, 'I didn't mean it to turn out like this…'

'**OUT!**' Mum snarled.

In slow-mo, Davey walked through the kitchen, where I saw Gwennol and Siriol waiting, and he got into his car.

'No!' Gwennol said, 'No you don't.'

Meekly, Davey handed over his keys, and Gwennol drove his Peugeot down the lane and away in the direction of Tywyn. I knew I would never see the old red 205 again.

Siriol let out a long, deep breath, then kissed Mum and came to me. She put her two small hands on my shoulders, kissed me on the cheek, then lightly on the mouth.

I touched my lips with my fingers. It was my first kiss.

e r God,' I said again, 'I know I keep asking you for stuff, but I don't know what else to do. And I know I never used to believe in you, but I figure that if you really did make the lake at Talyllyn, and the sea and the cliffs, then you might be able to fix it that Chinks is alive. Amen. Please. Save him. Amen.'

I said this quietly as I stood in the lane.

Mum was rooted to the exact spot in the sitting room where she had finished yelling at Davey. Suddenly I noticed that her whole body was shaking, slightly at first, then violently, as if she was putting it on.

'Mum!' I said.

She flattened herself to the wall and slid down into a sitting position on the floor.

'Has he gone?' she asked, her teeth chattering.

'Really and truly. Gwennol drove him away.'

'I was so afraid of him Joel.'

I fetched her long coat and draped it over her like a blanket. 'In the end he looked more scared of you than you are of him.'

'Why did I put us through all this?' she shivered.

'Probably because you needed someone to love you,' I said, 'like I need Chinks.'

That was too much for us both, and we cried together like a couple of abandoned kids, a pair of orphans who don't know where to go.

'I love you,' she sobbed.

'And I love you,' I replied. Then I lifted my face to her and wiped my eyes with the sleeve of my sweatshirt, 'What I said earlier, I didn't mean it. I do forgive you.'

My mobile rang in my pocket. Could it be? Please let it be.......

'Hello!' I said urgently.

'This is Her Majesty's Coastguard, Tywyn.'

Please God, please, ...

'We've got some very good news. And it's on its way to your farm, wrapped in a blanket, and very hungry.'

I held out the phone to Mum, because I couldn't speak for weeping.

'Thank you, thank you, bless you,' she said and hung up.

Chinks came home in a rescue vehicle. It had red flashing lights and fluorescent stripes, and the men were wearing reflective suits. The red flashes threw light onto our cottage walls, and the trees around us.

Siriol came out of her house like a bullet from a gun.

'Mrs Tillyard?' the driver asked.

'Yes, yes,' Mum beamed.

The driver opened the rear doors and unlocked a box, then lifted an armful of woollen and aluminium blankets. I was at his side, and parting the rough fabric, I saw two dark, shining eyes. He was exhausted, but Chinks licked my hand weakly.

'He needs to see a vet,' the man said, and Gwennol pulled up in a taxi bang on cue.

We all squeezed into our kitchen. Gwennol brought his veterinary case from his own van, the rescue men placed Chinks carefully on the table, and I stroked him so very gently.

He was frighteningly cold.

Gwennol was swift and alert. He checked the heart and breathing and looked worried, 'Open the Aga Caitlin, the warming oven at the bottom.'

Mum did as she was told.

'Siriol, fetch the fleecy blanket from my van.'

Siriol did.

He spread the fleece in the bottom of the warming oven, un-wrapped Chinks, and placed him inside. Then he almost closed the oven door.

'Won't that cook him?' the driver asked.

'Best thing for him,' Gwennol replied, 'This is how I've

saved hundreds of premature lambs on these hills. Invaluable things, range cookers.'

'Will he make it?' Siriol asked desperately.

I couldn't speak.

'He has every chance, his breathing is steady, and his heart's strong, I think he'll pull through,' Gwennol replied.

'How did you find him?' Mum asked the driver.

Siriol put the kettle on, and that's when Mum fainted, fell flat on the floor like a collapsing deckchair.

Gwennol was brilliant, he sat Mum down at the kitchen table, put her head between her knees, and she came round very quickly.

'Sorry,' she said, 'it came over me so suddenly, I haven't eaten since this morning, and oh, that's what I need,' she said as Siriol set a huge cup of tea in front of her. It was her special mug that says HANDS OFF THIS TEA IS MINE. I gave it to her for Mothering Sunday.

Siriol had made tea for both the rescue men and everyone sat down.

Gwennol and I squatted on the floor beside the Aga, and he checked Chinks every couple of minutes. He was warming up. I listened to the man, but never took my eyes off the gap in the open Aga door. I could see the white fur, and in my head I kept saying, 'Please, please, please live!'

The Driver began, 'We were searching for over an hour before we had any luck. But we knew we were in the right place because we'd had a call from the police. A couple of walkers had reported seeing a man and a Jack Russell Terrier on the cliff path near Upper Borth. I don't want to upset you, but they saw a man pick up the dog and throw it over the edge.'

I squeezed my hand into the oven and smoothed Chinks'

soft head.

'We kind of knew that,' Mum said blankly.

'But although we combed the coastline in that area, there was no sign of him. The current's strong there, and we figured he may have been washed downstream towards Aberystwyth. The tide was high, so we were hopeful the dog would have fallen into the water, rather than onto rocks – which would have been disastrous from a height of seventy feet.

'It was a seagull that saved him really. We'd trawled up and down the coastline several times, and we reckoned the dog couldn't have survived in the water for that length of time. Suddenly my colleague spotted a gull on a ledge about five metres up. It was a Kittiwake, flapping at something, which we thought was another, bigger gull.

'My mate called, 'Hey Euan, that's not a gull,' and we took the RIB ashore.

'The white object was your dog, perching on the rocky ledge, and right beside the Kittiwake nest, which is why the bird was giving him a hard time. It didn't take us long to hoist ourselves up and bring him to safety. He was soaking wet, and shivering with fright and cold - he must have been in the water for a long time. But he's obviously a tough one.'

The rescue man sipped his tea.

'Thank you,' was all Mum said.

Just then a familiar whine came from the Aga.

Gwennol opened the door, 'Aha! Welcome back to life mate! I think he's ready for a bite to eat now Jo-Jo.'

At the beginning, I said you mustn't feel sorry for me, and now you definitely mustn't.

Because I'm having the best summer of my whole life by far.

Chinks has made an amazing recovery. Gwennol visited him every day for a week, and since then I've spent every minute with Siriol and Chinks. We've climbed Cadair Idris, rowed on the lake, and ridden Duncan on the Talyllyn railway. We run for miles on the white sands of Aberdyfi beach – although Chinks never goes in the sea any more, and if we throw his ball in by mistake, we have to fetch it for him, while he barks excitedly at the edge.

If it's possible, I love him even more now than I did before, and we can't bear to be apart. He sleeps on my bed, we watch TV together, and he follows my bike wherever I go.

And – embarrassing – it turns out that Uncle Gwennol fancies my Mum. Really fancies her. It makes me and Siriol cringe, but they've started holding hands, and going out for meals on their own.

Apparently Gwennol is in remission, which means the cancer is far less bad than it was.

I asked Mum the other day, 'Is he still going to die soon?'

And she said, 'Joel, what a way to put it! There's no reason to suppose he won't live longer than me.'

Siriol and I took a picnic to her den last week.

I was rolling round in the bracken with Chinks, me tugging on one end of an old rope, him winning on the other end.

Siriol was lying on the ground, looking at the sky and chewing on a blade of grass. Out of nowhere she announced, 'I reckon your Mam and Uncle Gwennol will get married. They might even have a baby!'

'Don't be ridiculous,' I replied, collapsing on the bracken beside her.

Chinks rested his chin on my stomach.

'Do you ever think about finding your real Dad now?' she asked me.

'Never think about him. Because a real Dad isn't a man who's related to you by biology, it's a man who lets you stay when you've got nowhere to go, and puts his arms round you when you're upset. And knows how to cure animals.'

'So you found him after all. Race you to the bikes,' she said.

Author's Note

If you have enjoyed this story, you might like to know that many of the places I've written about are real. I fell in love with Talyllyn lake, Cadair Idris mountain and the Welsh coast on my first childhood visit 35 years ago.

You can trace Joel's journey to the lake by car, and you'll see the landmarks just as he did; take the A487 from Machynlleth through Corris.

Siriol's farm is real, but is private property, and everything about the lake is just as I have described, and has remained the same since my childhood. You can drive to Tywyn along the route of Morgan's bus, and see Joel's school too. Best of all, you can ride on Duncan (who is Douglas underneath), on the Talyllyn railway which runs from the coast, through Abergynolwyn, and up to Nant Gwernol.

And Chinks is a very real dog, though he has a different name, and he really did fall into the sea, where he was rescued by the Ministry of Defence Police Marine Unit.

Although the characters are fictitious, they, and Joel's story owe much to the real people of this beautiful part of Wales.

ACKNOWLEDGEMENTS

My sincere thanks to;

The staff and management of Tynycornel Hotel Talyllyn, for
their hospitality, and advice on the language,
The Talyllyn railway - staff and website,
Annie, Fran and Barbara for your encouragement,
Peter and Alison – please keep praying!
Everyone at Stickleback for making this possible,
And Maddy and Jim – for allowing me to run away with Joel
and Chinks.

Also by Helen Wilkinson

THE MISSING PEACE

"This book, aimed at 8-12 year olds, is a fascinating read and has a 'can't put it down' quality. The characters come to life from the first page. Set in the seaside holiday village of Dunwich, the book is tightly structured, intriguing and with a great twist at the end. I *thoroughly* recommend this book." Marion Field

"Wow! What a book! A beautiful story that hangs in the mind and heart for days after reading it. Helen really gets inside a child's mind and the mystery lasts right to the end."

Jennifer Rees-Larcombe

PETER'S DAUGHTER

Her peaceful life has been blown apart by a stranger. She's Susannah, Peter the fisherman's daughter, lost to history for 2,000 years until 21st century Ben; archaeologist and atheist – digs up a shard, and gives up everything to find her.

"Awesome, atmospheric. I cannot praise the author enough."

Authentic Media

"Peter's Daughter is beautiful."

Jonathan Aitken